PAMARTY VENKATARAMANA

The Whispering Star

**A BOOK OF
MODERN, MYSTICAL
SHORT STORIES**

novum pro

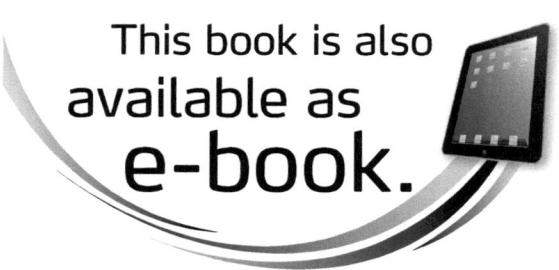

This book is also available as e-book.

www.novum-publishing.co.uk

© 2021 novum publishing

ISBN 978-3-99064-344-0
Editing: Ashleigh Brassfield, DipEdit
Cover photos: Vivilweb,
Ryhor Bruyeu | Dreamstime.com;
Lavanya Maddala
Cover design, layout & typesetting:
novum publishing
Internal illustrations: Lavanya Maddala
Author's photo:
Pamarty Venkataramana

www.novum-publishing.co.uk

1.

Smile of God !

It was the early sixties of the twentieth century. All the world had been witnessing a realignment of maps, lands and countries. The League of Nations had become a flop. The two great wars of civilisation had taken their toll on all humanity. There was no victor nor vanquished. Acrimonious debates were no longer in fashion. Animosities had died down – almost finished off! The United Nations Organisation was the new hope of a new world.

He was the Head of a world Religion. Not an order, but whole races followed the Religion religiously. He had mastered the scriptures, read the tracts off dimly lit library tables throughout long hours of uncertain times, even as a youth. Soon, Dame Luck propelled him to the highest seat of position in the Religion. He was a Demi-God to his council of advisers and the mammoth administrative system his post demanded him to preside over. To the blind adherents though, he was God in person ...

As the huge jumbo jet landed on the soil of an ancient foreign land named India (of whose glorious past in the ages gone by he had read in chronicles written by ancient Mariners, priests and apostles who had sailed the stormy, deep seas), he felt a trepidation come over his Being. Was it fear of unknown snake-charmers? Was it of great royal Bengal tigers reported to be prowling around the deer, dainty peacocks and the prancing hordes of monkeys? Or, was it of some alien culture, which was termed pagan-worship by his kinsmen, but which, in truth, and to his personal knowledge, was an even higher form of worship of Universe, of Life and of Supreme Soul?

He murmured a prayer in an ancient Roman language and the sense of relief returned him to a buoyant present state of mind.

In God We Trust ...!
These were the magic words of consolation that always emboldened him in times of trepidation, guilt, sadness, remorse and fear. As they did now ...

He, more than anybody else that followed the remarkable religion he was currently the living head of, was aware of his existence as a mere mortal on Earth – susceptible, vulnerable and prone to weaknesses, illness and temptations. Much venerated as he was...

The 'His Worship', 'His Holiness', 'His Exalted Highness' – titles charmed the utterers of the words and the myriad Believers of the myth of the Head of Religion being the carrier of the Spirit of God Almighty! But it merely brought a faint twitch to his facial nerves. The high crown he had to wear, and the long staff, heavily laden with precious stones, were the weighty adornment of his prime status.

There was a motley group of saffron clad Hindu priests, of whom he had only read in the books and translated versions which he had access to, come to life, standing before a string of saree-clad young women holding large rose-garlands in their hands. The protocol officer of his Western headquarters had cautioned him against kissing them or hugging them in warm embrace, but to bow low and let them garland his short neck. He was actually a diminutive frame as a human figure, but the daunting, treasured chapel, cloak, crown, staff and crystal ball held in his palms as a ready weapon against any ferocious tiger who crossed his path lent him the image of a towering figure of majesty!

There were even three huge, black elephants with umbrellas decorated with velvet clothes and silken garments trumpeting a welcome to him. He let the damsels garland him. Resisted an impulse to plant a few blessings on their rosy cheeks. They certainly appeared to be the celestial maidens one read about in ancient Indian folklore. Was it that their well draped and graceful persona added a magical charm to their natural beauty? Well, it wasn't right to be flirtatious on such a solemn State occasion, in any case.

After all, this State visit was aimed at nurturing, adopting and gaining control over a vast territory of the world, stretching from the grand Himalayas down south to where the three seas – the Indian Ocean, Bay of Bengal and the Arabian Sea – met…

As local bigwigs escorted by turbaned, giant looking moustached soldiers and representatives of his own religion began to come to where he was seated, on a replica of his throne back home, and kissed the back of his outstretched palm, he let a mysterious smile play on his lips.

Inwardly, he mused to himself at the ingenuity exhibited by his chief caretaker, a widowed aristocratic lady who forced him to wear a pair of translucent gloves in order that germs passing from those who came in contact with His Worship's hand did not harm him, as they do all other normal human beings...

Irreverent am I? He looked askance at himself as the huge diamond ring presented to him by the Sheriff of Bombay reflected his face, as though from a movie projector.

No, the love and adulation exhibited by this country's people was of an order he had not seen anywhere before, in all his travels around the civilised globe...

Just as he was getting up to say a mass prayer, a little, fair-skinned boy of seven walked up to him, holding the finger of the Sheriff, and gifted the world's most powerful leader of thought and religion a beautiful, red rose!

The fragrance was mesmerisingly pleasant, fresh, and transported him, as other aphrodisiacs always did to people. He condescendingly whispered aloud, "God bless you little one!"

At once, the lad looked him in the eyes and spoke in pure English: "Have you seen God?"

The non-plussed Head of Religion, simply amazed, smiled dazedly and gave a few furtive glances at the child, even as the Sheriff turned pale and white in fear. The latter mumbled that the boy was his youngest son and that he be forgiven for whatever offensive words he might have said.

The Head simply gaped, doubly surprised at the apologies being rendered by the father of one who had actually given him the words of Enlightenment!

After the brief three-day, whirlwind tour, as he was to depart for his homeland, the Police Commissioner informed the Sheriff of the City that his little son was asked to be brought immediately under strictly guarded, secret escort. The Family members were shocked and frightened, for theirs was the oldest Brahmin family of the region and held in greatest respect by one and all. It was a slur on the dignity of an entire dynasty if one chit of a child could recklessly hurt or insult a visiting dignitary, and that too of none other than the revered Head of the world's most powerful, reigning religion!

But they had to honour the request.

The child was sent in his finest linen to meet the Head of Religion, an honoured guest of the whole country!

What transpired then was a beautiful moment for all who were privy to it: The Head kneeled down as the little young boy approached him, took his little palm and kissed it as though it was a holy grail, and placed his hand above the child's head and said a prayer lasting a few minutes, which none present there could understand nor remember.

The boy was sent back to his house along with an inspector of police. The visiting dignitary was given a ceremonial send-off, this time with a contingent of finest horsemen doing an equestrian display. Music bands played live.

The atmosphere was one of merriment.
Nirvana!
Moksha!
Salvation!

All were words. God bless you, we all say, some more often than others; many more choose not to acknowledge the presence of God, or any superpower of the mighty Universe.
But, to those who do keep saying as they breathe – "God bless you!"

Have you ever seen God?

Or, felt the presence of an unseen, Almighty, super-natural God?

Yes, to the curious ones, that young man in this tale grew up in the six decades since, and I had the chance to meet him in person and explain to him of the presence of God, godliness and goodness of God in being as vividness: seen yet unseen; untouched but felt; worshipped but evasive in a sceptical environment of scientific temper, short tempers and haughty attitudinal behaviour of lesser mortals that abound in our societies, today...

It takes a lot of understanding to grasp the essence of presence of God in one and all animate as well as inanimate objects of Mother Nature!

Self-realisation comes as a shock. Numbing all vanity. Invoking good conscience. Peace, serenity and bliss only follow such a defining moment of our lives.

Praise the Lord!
AUM...
Love and Peace...

Have you seen God present in your actions, thoughts, neighbourhood? As the Head of yore, let enlightenment dawn upon us instantly: love alone merits a life.

2

Star of love

She was as energetic at eighty-five years of age as when she was eight years old. All the wrinkles added grace and light to her beautifully chiselled features. A smile played perennially on her face, and the glint in her marble-like blue eyes added to the aura she projected around herself!

And she carried herself with the demeanour befitting the head of a living family tree of fifty members, ranging from tiny toddlers, to youths, to middle-aged people, to 'senior citizens'. In a way, she was a union of several wills, to a single, whole and undivided will. They all adored her strong presence, celebrated life in her jovial, bubbly company.

And today was a very special day for her. Every Christmas day brought with it memories of her own Santa Claus.

***

The old man still had the striking features of the handsome soldier who had joined the armed forces as a reluctant youth, on the insistence of his grandfather, who had fought in the Great War of Civilisation but had, over the years, risen to become a Field Marshal and honourably retired from service of the Motherland. The price of fame, though, in changed times, has been the acquisition of fabulous wealth by his kith and kin, but each of his children and grandchildren were so caught up in their own worldly pursuits that they had to cross the oceans to meet one another once every few years. The widower loved his glass of rum and stack of books; a round of golf with the old boys or the odd game of tennis at the Club helped him stay fit as a fiddle. What cost was all the Wealth and Prosperity attained in the name of a fragile Peace after all those bitter Wars? This was the nagging question which plagued his mind every waking hour in recent times.

And so, he was now flying out to spend the Christmas with the men of the Fifth Regiment, from which he had graduated to become a superior Officer, winning his first Sword of Valour. Even as he looked across the aisle from his window seat on the flight taking him to Madras, he espied a little girl with blinking eyes, clutching on to her Barbie handbag, taking a seat in the other row. No one seemed to escort the little child, who appeared to be no older than seven years. The airhostesses were fluttering about like butterflies but as mechanical as worker bees. They did not bother to answer the child's repeated pleas for a glass of water; nor were they attending to his buzzer-call.

He winced aloud: was this the era of carelessness he and thousands of other soldiers had sacrificed their lives for? Sending out a prayer to the souls of all his men who were martyred in the call of duty, the old gentleman officer soon found his musings interrupted by the pilot's in-flight announcement that they would be landing in a short while.

As expected, during deplaning, he and the little girl were overtaken by all their co-passengers, who appeared in a greater hurry to get off the plane. Still holding the Barbie-doll handbag, she tentatively ambled towards the exit gate. Noticing that a painting-box had dropped out of her hands, the pink-faced old man bent down to pick it up and hand it to her. She gave a smile of surprise and gratitude at the same time. And, in a sing-song voice, she said, "Thank you, Uncle!"
He turned beetroot red at the courteous little greeting. The gratitude for old-world manners rang loud and clear. As they both ambled towards the baggage-claim area, the two chatted like two long lost friends. She was visiting her auntie's place alone for Christmas because her father was a very busy surgeon who could not afford a holiday, and her mother had to stay back to cook his meals and keep house. This was her first trip alone. She was a topper in her class and aimed to become a police officer when she grew up. There were so many problems with law & order in society, she declared. She also informed him that he resembled the picture of the Field-Marshal whose portrait adorned the Hall of Fame in her school library, and giggled long and loudly.

The old man joined in the merriment.

Just as they were parting ways on her sighting her Aunt, Uncle & cousins, who had come to welcome her home, on an impulse the old man with the pink smile thrust his long hands into a corner of his briefcase, took out a small golden cover and, along with a box of Swiss chocolates, handed it over to the sweet little creature, planting a peck on her forehead.

With a mock-harsh tone, he said: "Officer, you shall not open this box before Good Old Santa Claus visits you tonight!"

The conspiratorial tone excited the child no end, and she held up a palm and said, "I promise you, Uncle!"

He felt a lump in his throat as their car disappeared into the traffic.

***

The clock struck twelve.

It was Christmas day again!

A solitary tear ran down her cheek.

She opened the golden box with her entire family of fifty gathered in the huge drawing room, seated by the fireplace and the beautiful Christmas Tree decorated with little bulbs of different colours. A bright photograph smiled at them all from beside the Christmas Tree.

"Oh, I am imprisoned in this world even eighty years from that date, Uncle!" she whispered. And, moved to tears, she gently opened the box which was presented to her by the Uncle who had endeared himself to all of her being and family; out popped a glistening Gold Medal with the inscription: "The Honoured First Field Marshal"! A golden star glistened, as the solitary star which directed the Three Magi on that fateful night, all those years ago on their way to the manger-crib of the son of God!

That was the most treasured possession of the grand old warrior, valued higher than any other valuable or asset which his kith & kin had been endowed with. He had said this in the last telephone conversation he had with the little girl, just after she had opened it at home. And her Uncle had called him, astonished at the amazing gesture of a noble man they had only read about in popular media and never imagined they would meet. All the elders were floored at his affable, honest voice expressing his sincerest wish to gift it to her whole-heartedly.

The next morning's news of the death of the Gentleman Soldier sent the household into a pall of gloom more intense than a whole nation felt. The little girl grew up into a little woman, who soon won laurels for her stellar role in rendering medical attention to soldiers on the battlefront and during peacetime. "Desi Florence Nightingale" they all named this Angel of Mercy, Compassion and Humanity!

The beautiful little infant, youngest member of her clan, holding out a tiny fist to touch the Gold Medal brought her back out of the reverie. A young grandnephew began to sing: "Jingle Bells, Jingle Bells, Jingle all the way…!"

She joyously cried, "Merry Christmas!"

3.

Star of Destiny!

A lanky old man ambled along India Gate. He had a round egg-head, with large ears that seemed to highlight its rotundness, and rimmed glasses adorning his frail yet glowing face; he had a constant smile on, though!

He had known Delhi to be a historic venue of many a political battle of warring hearts, witty minds, devious brains and dim-wits across the ages of its existence. The last he had walked the pathways was just before his assassination on that fateful morning of January 30th. The topography had changed drastically, and the lifestyles, too, had transformed dramatically! No longer was it a serene city of lush green trees and sleepy old villages clustered around the hub of all capital activity! The greenery was confined to a select corner, whilst tar roads with motor vehicles of all foreign make were racing one another, only to be humbled in the traffic jams created as a result of the mad rush. Nobody seemed to give way to anyone. Sign boards were hung at the wrong places and there was certainly a hell of a lot of going around to be done if one were a tourist, or an out of time visitor, like himself!

He was a man with a mission.

He recollected how, in his earlier life, as a young student, he was made to atone for his sin of meat-eating abroad upon his return to his native land; how he wed a young bride; how he mobilised strength to act as a galvanising force to the local Indian community in Durban, where bubonic plague struck, killing thousands of people, and his compatriots were a wholly unorganised lot; how he, though a barrister, was thrown out of a first class railway compartment, although he held a valid first class ticket, because of the colour of his skin; how he was felt it an affront to his dignity and self-respect and returned to his homeland, India; how he sensed the crying pleas of people at large in the land of many princely states, for wealth and grandeur, for freedom from the foreign yoke; how the tyranny of a sizeable number of wicked Englishmen led to rebellion and revolt from the people of a most hospitable, loving land, which had let the East India Company plunder its riches – like rare gems, gold, silver, jewellery, spices, condiments, silks and countless other treasures; how the divide and conquer policy of the foreign colonialists had led to a break in harmony among people professing different religions as a private faith in life; how he led the salt satyagraha and the countless fasts and non-violence movement; how the entire country was inspired by his writings in the Young India, a mouthpiece; how Sir A.O. Hume and Annie Besant of the Theosophical society had impressed him; how the Congress party began to see divisions of thought and Jinnah began to seek self-glory; how the Vijayawada session of the party and the Round Table Conference in London had helped steer the cause of the Indian Nation; how Jawaharlal, his good friend, had a soft spot for certain people and regions whilst Netaji Subhas Chandra Bose founded the Azad Hind Fauj army on the Burma front and Sardar Vallabhbhai Patel, C.K. Rajagopalachari and several other statesmen accepted his ideology of non-violence movement and boycott of foreign spun yarn; how eventually he had to relent to the partition of the motherland by foreign rulers, who had the last laugh by dividing the entire Indian sub-continent as they left under extreme protests against oppression, wickedness, tyranny, subjugation, slavery and internecine wars occasioned by the diplomacy of the governors sent by Her Majesty of Great Britain; how sad he was on hearing news of riots on the western and eastern frontiers; how he was shot by a most unlikely assassin, even as he was participating in a prayer meeting!

Yes, he did fulfil the destined purpose of his birth in that lifetime, when on August 15th, 1947, at the stroke of midnight, India won freedom and joined the comity of free countries in a new world order!

Now, on this the second day of October 2013, the anniversary of his birth was being celebrated by a nation grateful to him, indebted to his steadfastness and focused strategy to free countless numbers of compatriots from the unbridled reign of terror – plunder, loot, murder and other unspeakable crimes – by foreign colonial rule. The Mahatma had set foot in flesh and blood in answer to the many prayers of anguished countrymen! He knew not what had transpired in the intervening decades after his death, but he knew that the cries for help rang loud and touched his soul, restless and never at peace since his ghastly murder…

He had been greatly influenced by his Guru, Acharya Vinoba Bhave, the founder of the Bhoodan Movement, which sought to distribute land for landless poor citizens and also fought against cow slaughter in India. Vinobhaji had revealed to him the essence of Bhagavad Gita, the Voice of Prophecy, Philosophy and Blessing of God (as revealed by Lord Sri Krishna to Arjuna, the warrior prince who had become depressed on noticing that all his adversaries in war were kith & kin, not strangers). By far, this was the most revealing part of the world's largest epic; the Mahabharata and its philosophy were metaphysical, an eye opener to deal with matters of life and death; birth and growth; good and bad; evil and punishment; conscience and crime; relatives and relationships, and every other conceivable facet of mankind – all comprised in eighteen chapters! It had taken him three long years of living at the Paunar Ashram to grasp the essence of the Gita and all it has to offer to every race, generation, and era of mankind! His character was moulded and redesigned by the knowledge of the innate principles of dharma (there still was no equivalent to this mighty Sanskrit word in any dictionary or religion of the world, he chuckled), and he was confident of it carrying him through any situation, age and era of societal existence!

Well, he gave a toothless, friendly smile to the soldiers and many tourists that gather around Raj Ghat, the memorial erected to honour his memory. But none seemed to acknowledge him: it was as if he did not exist at all. This puzzled him before he heard the playful laughter of a few little children from across the lush, green turf area; and as he approached them, he noticed at least half a dozen look-a-likes of himself! The youngest was a child of twelve years, and the oldest was nearly sixty years old: all were dressed in his famous, frugal wear and painted with silver, and a few passers-by were dropping coins into the bowls they held in one hand while the long, walking stick was in another hand. No wonder: the soldiers guarding his memorial and the other visitors assumed he was another imposter of himself!

What an irony, he mumbled to himself, and he took a stroll along the breath-taking landscape of the structure designed to honour him and all he had stood for, in that life.

He heard a foreign couple discuss about Martin Luther King of America, and then of a certain Nelson Mandela of South Africa (a land dear to a certain portion of his past lifetime, he mused!), who was acclaimed as a Gandhian and was said to be heartily alive even as a vast number of his well-wishers were prepared for obits a few months back: ah, the world still has its share of evil folk?

So, these were television cameras and could beam and flash news in real time? He looked around for a newspaper, but a school student informed him of Internet technology and iPads and smartphones being in vogue. He also learnt of some pleasing news: India, his dear motherland, had scaled heights in space, scientific research, technology and education frontiers.

The Mahatma was filled with tears and almost wept inconsolably when he learnt of brain drain, of agriculture being neglected, of rampant corruption permeating administration at different levels, of criminals reigning in politics, of the rise in lawlessness and changing societal mores, including the collapse of the joint family system, of increased consumerism leading to national leaders sporting best world brands from overseas, of everything undesirable, unthinkable and unimaginable taking place in the country he fathered, so to speak!

He then noticed that the sun had set, and dusk had fallen. A set of artificial lights illuminated the area. Soon, he was ushered out, as the gates were being closed.

To where should he turn his footsteps at this hour and in this place, he asked himself. Of course, to the traditional dinner the President must be hosting on the auspicious day, he answered. He found his way there, only to be halted by gun toting security personnel. They checked him for any explosives he may be carrying on his person, ignoring his protests, pointing out to his loin cloth attire.

An affable-looking older guard gave a friendly smile and told him "*bapu*, everybody takes Mahatma's name and apes his words... Today, it is fashionable for even terrorists to wear Gandhiji's attire and trouble us, so please understand... And, yes, there is no party today. His Excellency has left abroad this afternoon on an official tour…"

The Mahatma then traced his path to the lawns of the Prime Minister's official residence, assuring himself of being able to meet the worthy successors of the constituent assembly of Free India. He was surprisingly redirected to the house of good old Jawaharlal Nehru's daughter's daughter in law, a foreigner turned Indian national, who it appeared was the de facto head of government, even though a bureaucrat turned politician was the prime minister *de jour*!

Oh dear, what a state of affairs has befallen on the nation called India!
As he stepped closer, an army officer saluted him and said, "*Bapuji*, I will let you in upon my personal guarantee. I will record you as my grandfather from the village. I only hope you will not create any problem in there!"

A light of hope glittered. The glint in Mahatma's eyes shone. He nodded and said, "Yes, my son… stay blessed!" And he was let in, escorted by two orderlies.

The huge lawn was filled with many sporting his trademark white cotton caps, but many others wore British tailored suits and not one donned khadi, he observed. A bevy of waitresses and team of waiters were fawning over the gathering. He was stunned to sense the stench of alcohol from a couple of passers-by! He had fought for total prohibition, in a cultural society needing sane, sober, hard workers. Rules and laws seemed to have undergone a vast change across these six decades that he was not alive on this earth!

Nobody appeared to respect his presence. All were speaking of a Madam Gandhi and her son, Mr. Gandhi. A frail looking foreign looking woman then came in and was followed by an older

Sardarji (a turbaned Sikh gentleman) a few steps behind her. A hush fell over the gathering. Then began the speeches, and every person, without exception, was praising the Gandhis of the day without a mention of his name or presence! There were parliamentarians of all political hues and shades, but none cast even a furtive glance at him, not even the press corps! Only the security personnel on duty seemed to give the Mahatma a glance, but their suspicious looks further saddened him: where was the India he and millions of freedom fighters had dreamt for, had fought for, had sacrificed for? Where was India, a land of wisdom and love? Where was India, the soul of earth? Why were his countrymen eyeing each other with suspicion? Where did the heritage and culture go? But he had heard, in the evening, of the Taj Mahal, the red fort and many other heritage structures being preserved. Was culture and heritage merely a site on the world wide web? Freedom won at enormous cost of life and lifetimes had no resemblance to their dreams, it appeared... No, he was always a man with an understanding of the world of humans... Humane existence was a must. Humanity looked up towards his teachings (influenced by the Bhagavad Gita, of course!), and yet his own nation was in turmoil.

India needed him. Now, more than ever before: Mahatma Gandhiji realised this.
And, leaning against an old Ashoka tree, on the lawns of the Memorial, the grand old man of non-violence and peaceful agitation in the world began to draw up a plan to battle the dark shadows which seemed to have shrouded his motherland.
What next?
Folks, I await too, with bated breath!
Long live non-violence! Long live Democracy!

4.

The Pole-Star

It was the day of the Big Bang: only one super star was left, shining bright in the open skies across the Milky Way, staying aloof and high above the rest of the glittering littler ones. He was the one and only Pole-Star!

Nobody had heeded his advice; all would ridicule his predictions and warnings of an impending danger. In fact, all the female stars would giggle and male stars smirk whenever they saw his luminous form rant and rave about safety, morality and a disciplined lifestyle to be incorporated into their clan of celestial forms. Even the constellations would turn a Nelson's eye to his imploring gaze!

Then came the fateful hour of the space system: there was a huge explosion, and all matter turned to dust; the molecules of space split in atomic fission and the fusion of striking meteors and sinking space debris converted the whole sky into one space-scape of cacophonous static, and the riot of unseemly colours and shades of space pollution resembled the flotsam and jetsam of convoluted mindsets... Large space objects became little, shiny starlets in a fraction of a millisecond, and the clear, golden sky suddenly turned dark, with twinkling dots of remnants of big stars merely speckling the stark reality of the careless neglect, recklessness and arrogance of the majority!

Only the one who was wise, kind, and energetic survived the holocaust... He, the Pole-Star, to this day, leads those who are willing to heed his directions, and enjoys the pride of place in the skies, over-shadowing the rest of the crowd. He remains the source of light for the umpteen numbers of poor dwellers down below, in the remotest corners of the planet Earth (the lone planetary piece which had enough water and air to keep it afloat and even let life spring into being in its unique atmosphere), and sends out the warmth of his presence to keep their heads high and chins low, with thoughts of another day – filled with hope, yearnings and love, of life!

As in the case of the Pole-Star, this writer shall continue to predict, interject and permeate through the finer senses of mankind – with, without or against your understanding of the gross reality!

Yes, let us all save Humanity by directing all Mankind towards the pathway of Divinity... Life is space itself; the lifetime is the universe; be the Pole-Star!

Only the Pole-Star can lead the weary travellers though the sand dunes on a cold desert night!

5.

A Shooting Star!

I always sought a window seat on the many air journeys I had to make, criss crossing the skies as a part of my flaming ambition to knit the world together in the love of letters. In the pre-Internet era, scores of rejection slips from famous publishing houses pulled the rug from beneath my feet, but in the digital age of self-publication and direct online sales, I was the engine driver, and my train of thoughts could reach out to all sorts of readers, from the remotest corners of the Earth! The response was spontaneous and fantastic. I no longer had to live on a loaf of bread for an entire twenty-four-hour cycle; in fact, I was now proudly sponsoring charity balls, dinners, and buying out a whole auditorium for musical shows of spastic and specially abled children, as well as adults! I no longer felt it shameful to walk miles on foot through the busy thoroughfares of the city of lakes: in fact, I began to enjoy the handshakes from strangers who recognised my face and frame from newspaper stories and television interviews, which became my avocation, it seemed, second only to writing – more prolific than before the moola poured into my kitty …

The chief reason for opting for a window seat was the delight and awe I felt upon espying other aeroplanes way below or up above my craft, seeming to resemble the sparrows and myna birds that would squeak, flutter and sing as they showed off their flight-prowess to us children, who would either race each other on the rough ground or play 'hide and seek' amidst the trees on campus.

Yet another passion was star-gazing, ever since childhood, which only instilled the curiosity to watch the glittering or paler stars as my plane soared away towards its destination, fuelled by jet engines but piloted with the autopilot technology of manmade computers!

My favourite route was the evening flight one takes to reach the national capital from the commercial capital of the country, especially on the new moon, or a full moon! All the celestial objects turned beings, and their rhapsodies of joy, and I would often wonder if indeed there were truth to the age-old theory that all those human beings who were good on earth during their lifetime would transcend the skies and turn into stars upon exit of the soul from their bodily forms! This did seem logical, because even as an adult and a world-renowned writer of substantial fame, I still failed to count the actual number of stars visible on the firmament of the sky, up above the mansions and skyscrapers...

Thus it came to be that, on one such evening's sojourn, I spotted a bright blue star alongside my window seat: being a teetotaller, I always refused the poor excuse of a meal that these low-cost airlines sold or supplied on the craft; besides, there was a lesser chance of being slighted by rude, ill-mannered hostesses. The explanation of my in-flight eating habits is necessary because those unaware of this fact would be prone to think that I had alcoholic drinks, one too many, and therefore had sighted this beautiful star firstly staring at me, then winking, then smiling and after that shooting alongside the plane – to be precise, exactly as my companion traveller would, in my company! – because I was drunk.

I was bedazzled of course, and as is my wont, I smiled back at her after casting a furtive glance around to see if anybody was watching me and my lovely companion outside the window! Oh, how I longed to hang my head out of the window and, if possible, shake a point of the Star! I began to grasp the significance of what was happening and in real time: I started communicating with her using my secretly honed skill of telepathy (with which I had, since my school days, spoken to the plants and the trees, the boulders and the clouds).

"Hello earthling, what are you gaping at me for?"

I bowed and replied, "At your stellar beauty!"

"Oh, you find me beautiful?" and she blushed a crimson red for a long moment.

"Yes!"

"But I find your Earth beautiful, and so do my co-stars from this and every other constellation in the sky! We watch you all day and night."

"My God!" I let out a gasp.

"You are a magnetic personality and so I am drawn towards your mind: we no longer can peep through the cumulus clouds, or the golden and cotton ones, even by sunlight's aid – the smog your settlements and inventions have spread has not only eroded the ozone layer, the ground level atmosphere too is wholly polluted. Even our star gaze fails to comprehend the short sightedness of you creatures, humans – they whom Almighty has bestowed with the greatest boon of intellect and native intelligence!"

I hung my head in shame, but without taking my eyes off her almost life size form (phew, what a way to compare a cosmic body with an earthly mind), lest I lose her presence.

"Why don't you write about this comment of mine in one of your tell-tale works? It is not a tall order, is it?"

"I will, your majesty!" I heard myself promise.

"Tell them all, the young and the older ones down below, that unless Earthlings begin to act wise and sensibly and stop further environmental degradation, not just bio-diversity or ecosystems, but we stars in the sky shall cease to exist for you all: just as you people cannot see us with bare eyes any longer due to the vapour of high-voltage lamps and mast-lights that blind you to the real lamps lit up above the world so high, similarly, we too will begin to forget your existence beneath all the filth and poisonous substances emitted, left, right and centre!"

On an impulse, I cast yet another of my furtive glances to the left, right and centre from the corners of my spectacles... None even seemed to notice my existence!

On the other hand, here was a celestial companion who had observed me watching her often during my regular flight trips, and who had condescended to meet me and speak with me too!

I again took a deep breath and mustered enough courage to ask her identity.

Quickly came the reply, "I am the lucky star."

"Whose?"

"Your lucky star… I am the one you will recognise anywhere in the universe, and in whatever chore you may be performing in your everyday lifestyle! There is one for every human being who is born on Earth. Whilst some take pride and joy in theirs, there are a multitude of masses that jump up and create an uproar when a child is born in some unknown household…few others do not bother even if the lucky star visits – they let go and lose out in life!"

I posed an innocuous sounding question. "Are you sailing with me all through life, oh my lucky star, or are you just visiting me on just this one journey?"

With a smile incomparable to even Michelangelo's or Raja Ravi Verma's paintings, she answered, "when a pair of human parents look at one another's eyes and find us, the stars in each other's eyes, we simply fly down to shelter the new-born baby, and once the infant is given a name to be known by, we respond to the call of thy very name; and alongside you we stand, through thick and thin; through the upheavals and downward spirals of life's journey…"

My mind raced, reminding me that hardly anybody nowadays was ever called by their complete, full christened name, and almost everybody appeared to be going about life with a lost face or putting on long faces; every second 'Earthlings' seemed to be in search of an identity, as well as a purpose for their very existence…!

"I am with you because you are forever utilising my presence in what your world of literature dubs as good conscience, gratitude and goodness… These are the three elements that comprise a heavenly being, created by God in God's own image, as your ancient scriptural texts say…"

"Amen!"

Did I say this, or was it the crackling voice over the in-flight address system which disturbed my concentration and resulted in me losing sight of my singularly beautiful travel companion, the blue star, my own lucky star?

A shooting star, I would now dare define, is one lucky star who is downed by mankind, which believes in artificial cloud-seeding for rainfall; in neon lamps of lighting up nights; clipped nicknames for given proper names; slang and abbreviated words in place of decent and wholesome sounding languages as means of communication!

In a nutshell, when mankind slips from natural kindness, the shell breaks and all go berserk and nuts: the best of science and technological use is often abused resulting in the inevitable destruction of a shining, lucky star... falling down from the skies...

A shooting star!

6.

Animals, not Humans!

The animals were gathered around the large clearing, which seemed to be the only area in the huge, thick forest of tall trees, short bushes, thorny creepers, fruit laden orchards with exotic smelling flowers of all hues and shades. It was an assembly of all the four-legged creatures as well as the winged avers that hovered around the world; of simple souls who never tried to outsmart Creation or Mother Nature Herself, like their counterparts, the human beings out there beyond their haven, seemed to indulge in doing day in and day out: no cloning, no capturing others for research, no tinkering with genetics to create hybrids – with due apologies to the monkeys of the forest world, these honest animals and birds never monkeyed around with their brains!

They had a single-minded purpose in life – be born, reared, and live by a food cycle laid out by Nature, grow up like there was no tomorrow, procreate to continue to live on after becoming food for a preying animal or upon natural death (which was rare) – not to be bothered with needing space or social networking tools nor artificial currencies and per capita income or insurance and savings schemes!

No, they were not schemers as the humans beyond the frontiers of their zone of universe. They never invented dogmatic religions, nor did they excommunicate their own for poverty or primitive ways and "lack of etiquette" at the table or on a dance floor! They did not conquer others' lands, nor did they engage themselves in gun-running, smuggling of narcotics or such other criminal activities that were banal even to the so-called civilisations of Mankind!

In short, the animals and birds of this particular greenwood forest were a contented lot, given the abundance of waterfalls, lakes, fruits, prey and even five perennial rivers, which quenched the thirst of the mighty predators as well as the docile squirrels and nubile deers. Their lord master, the mighty Lion, was their hero, and he in turn was a wise ruler who always counselled his wife, the huge sweet beautiful lioness, to be caring and thoughtful in pouncing upon the prey, which was the food she provided her master and their dozen cubs. He would organise an annual sports Olympiad of sorts, to nurture and hone the native abilities and natural skills of the leopards, the rabbits, the pigeons, the snakes, and the owls too. And there was the bi-monthly song competition for the parrots and the cuckoos, the koel birds, the nightingales, and the hyenas alike. Besides, the majestic ruler also had a novel way to feed the lesser beings, the docile cows, lambs and little sparrows. He would allow his leftover mutton and flesh-feed to be given to the hamlet of bullocks, and in turn, these tilled a large patch of land for grass to grow and in turn, the grass eating docile members of this animal family too had plentiful to eat, masticate and chew upon. There were very few instances now of death by starvation and healthy preys resulted in healthy predators. All in all, an excellent win-win situation!

They had no clocks nor wrist watches. The sun was the clock. When sunlight showed and sun rays peered through the dense, tall thicket of trees, it was dance hours. When the sun set or rainwater trickled through, it was sleep hours. No sense of being late nor early for an appointment with their kith and kin; never was there any fear of speeding trucks or spoilt, drunken brats behind the wheel of a vehicle running over an innocent pedestrian or a hopping grasshopper, a kangaroo or mongoose, either!

Utopia – this would have been the label a human philosopher would have given to this region of planet Earth!

The air was filled with poignant silence and a sense of animated suspense filled all the members of the assembled gathering.

Why?

Their lord master, the mighty emperor, their beloved Lion King, was going to announce that "all animals must turn vegetarian, for it was wrong to kill a fellow being, and why must animals turn into human-like beasts?" This news had trickled through the grapevine, of which the fox and the parrots, as well as the baboons and the peacocks, were integral parts. Even as plant eating animals rejoiced at the new jungle law in the making, those who breathed air only to feed on less powerfully endowed animals began to hold heated conversations amongst their hordes over the entire fortnight leading to the day of the annual general meeting. So kind was their ruler that he never convened an extraordinary general meeting for even the best of his brainwaves: a stickler for decorum, he awaited the scheduled day of their annual general meeting to place his new proposition for an equitable, sin-free land before his subjects!

The wily fox would bow to the huge oxen with pseudo-respect, while he would incite the cheetahs and the leopards by whispering into their silken ears, "Why don't you compulsorily retire the old chap, our senile lion, and learn a line or two from those crafty human beings – chair by rotation; once a flesh-eater, always a flesh-eater; I will moot your name for succeeding him to the throne!" and so on and so forth, trying to instigate a revolution of sorts in the otherwise peaceful land of unequally endowed but equally existing creatures!

The black cat with green eyes was his sidekick, and he purred in support – "Oh my, isn't he like that Indian emperor, Ashoka, who conquered all other lands, but when he faced defeat at the hands of a princess, had a change of heart and embraced the religious doctrine of another prince before him, who had married but deserted his wife, son and subjects in search of peace? He ordered all his ablest generals to turn monks, and the net result? The Huns and the Mongolians, the Turks, the Moghuls and the Brits, the Dutch and the Portuguese and, more recently, the terrorists and the nomad raiders have all been attacking a mighty land of vast population, merely because they changed the doctrine of life into that of "non-violence, non-alignment, and vegetarianism" and ancient rituals of longevity and happiness began to be viewed as pagan worship and idolatry... Oh, the history of man is rife with the ignorant riding rough over time tested, ageless wisdom... Are we turning as beastly as them humans?!"

As the elephants trumpeted, trunks up in the air, the Lion King ambled in and sat on the high turf laid with green grass, and all those assembled bowed in reverence and let out their respective, individualistic roars of greeting!

After an hour or so, they all got tired by the exercise, it appeared, and a blanket of silence enveloped the gathering.

His Majesty smiled and began to roar gently – "friends, animals, birds, trees, rivers and my beloved spouse, my lioness... I have the honour and the privilege of leading you all into the era of peace and plenty; no more killing and hunting; no more human-like existence; let us all become more humane than those humans out there in the wild jungle of concrete sky-scrapers and pollution spilling jets... Of course, those of us born wild by nature can change Nature itself by our will power. If a land like those Indians can have a secular state and yet provide for reservations for minorities; if they can call themselves a single Republic and yet go about butchering and dividing their borders; if they can survive without ample food, housing and basic amenities for a population one billion strong; if they can survive the onslaught of the corrupt, crooked and wicked few in the name of an unseen Almighty God, cannot we too begin to cultivate the taste of those diet-conscious few to overcome our natural yearning for the carcasses of fellow animals and instead eat nutritious, calorie-filled, hygienic plant leaves to lead a longer life in this heaven on earth? This would also please our census figures, and our mortality rate will drastically change...

"... If our population increases with this non-violent method, won't we outnumber those beastly humans who are far outpacing us in both methods of violence and lifestyles? If they are becoming more shameless and cruel by the day, why can't we outshine them in intellect, in reforms, and reform our way of life? If those human beings are fasting, ceasing to procreate by virtue of same gender wedlock, and such societal mores keep lessening their human sense of being higher beings than us, must we not re-think of a master plan to outwit our foes? No more do we need to dread the GPS-tagging or hunters' scary traps and baits...

"Young and old, all of us are animals, born alike, and since we all end up alike through death, by whatever factor caused, why should we not also learn to live alike, as equals and equally alike in food habits, and religiously adhere to the simple rule of being proud as a striped zebra or hopping kangaroo; a dancing peacock with all plumes in display, or my beautiful spouse, Her Majesty, the Lioness who is like a Mother to you all…?"

The Lion king glanced at his spouse, and did he imagine her blushing in joy, or was it at the apparently visible flattery he always indulged in while taking key decisions on matters of the State? … Well, his amusement was drowned out by the huge cheers that went up from the crowd.

Three cheers to the animal kingdom!

They always endorsed their ruler's decisions!

So much like human governance styles of late…or, is it unlike mankind's own sense of thoughts, discerning ability or differentiation prowess?

7

The Story Star!

The aliens had a star among them: she would regale them with tales of all types and genre; if on one elliptical orbit of their space-land, it was a story of heroic deeds by fore-fathers from that ancient, lost planet called 'Earth'; on another plane of time, it would be the saga of pre-Earth period mythological characters from that divine land called 'Bhaarat'!

While the elders gathered in keen amusement, youngsters of the race kneeled down to beat her gravitational pull – all were drawn to this singularly gifted star of their clan! Be it suspense or horror, humour or sarcasm, comedy or tragedy, earthly or unearthly, she had the gift of the gab… nay, of a brain filled with grey matter, and her proud mother always declared triumphantly that she was the only Space Mom with a daughter who had fifty heads put onto one lovely pair of shoulders!

Then came the anniversary of the creation of their space-land, i.e. the time slot of space when one long continuum of matter collided with all the grey shades of matter which corrupted mankind's orderly lifestyle, resulting in a final bang that ended a most lovely species, largely due to its own mischievous and even sinister ways of philandering with Nature using unnatural, illogical, crooked logic! All sense of right and wrong was lost; ethics and societal mores got distorted; shades of grey and yellow substituted red blood and blue eyed characters in literature; minds became molasses of technological multiple entendre and hearts became pit stops for bull fights among a supposedly civilised race of enlightened folk; children became adults at tender age, only a little over toddler-stage; adults grew senile by thirty years of age; manners and etiquette came to be regarded as arcane and pre-historic ways of the primitive, primate-like oldies; food was fast dished out of a machine and gulped in a jiffy, washed down by synthetic substance substituting for old-world water; sleep was minimal as each tried to outdo one's own dubious record of staying awake and winning war games or scoring points on a gaming toy-set; no longer was holy matrimony or reproduction of the species an 'in' thing, but cloning of animals, atomic molecules and live-in by the same gender became the sine qua non for nations to be dubbed as 'humane', 'modern' or 'advanced'!

On that fateful occasion, all of the lone space-land which flew out as debris from a shattered, living planet and landed on the edge of the spatial time-zone to stay put as a remnant of the golden era of evolution of life and matter in the galaxy popularly known to chroniclers as 'the Milky Way' paid their respects to this star-woman, whom they considered to be the saviour of their lives and souls;: yes, they saluted her presence and always bowed their radiant, rotund, shining grey heads and smiled with their valentine-shaped red hearts... And, they do a reprise of all the tales she tells throughout those leap years of doing nothing but smiling, breathing, singing, dancing, listening, sleeping, dreaming, awakening and living on for eternity as immortal beings of a blessed space-land!

Why?

She was the lone woman on earth who, in those hard, trouble and strife-filled final days of the beautiful planet Earth, would stay in a far corner of the mightiest nation of the times and utilise the outsourced services of a few from the oldest nation of all times; day and night diligently assimilating the tales of the young and the old; the girls and the womenfolk; the lads as well as the wise men; of space fiction and of real, true stories; of inspirational classics as well as the dramatic, adventurous ones; of fantasy and adventure; and of love, romance and human interest stories! A one-woman army, she helped knead the dough of story-telling mindsets and knit their tales into a common platform that they all fondly referred to as story star dot com!

It was the readers and authors that were prolific about her idea of 'opening up minds' and 'pouring out one's heart's content' who were fortunate to miss the apocalypse which was predicted, prophesied and debated for ages, but which, when it eventually visited, caught all unaware and unprepared for the unleashing of its fury and fervour or the speed and alacrity with which it took vengeance on the low-brows and the high-brows of society alike!

Thanks to a single individual with a soul, all those 'believers' of a nobler lifestyle called 'storytelling' were saved on judgment day: a time of reckoning truth imbibed by every scriptural text worth its following, and justice measured not by reading Fifty Shades of Grey or indulging in yellow journalistic pursuits on one's smart devices, but by the yardstick of compassion, love, kindness, mercy, understanding, sacrifice, sharing and every other such blue-blooded attribute of nobility!

Long live stars of the space-land!
Long live the story star!
Long live the stars!

8

Arms to Alms!

The forlorn figure lay huddled in a crouched position, teeth rattling, fists squeezed in a bid to ward off the aches of the biting chill of the early winter's night. The huge lamppost beneath which he parked himself all year long was the oldest of the many ornate pillars which still lined the outer boundary of the city's finest green park. Being an image of suffering, with his unkempt beard, marble like blue eyes and mustard grey hair ruffled, mounted on a weather-beaten face of wrinkles and agony writ large, he was the only vagabond from whom the beat constables never demanded a bribe or a salute, the latter when they were in a drunken stupor and preyed upon the beggars on the streets and such other discards of an unequal society to assuage their egotistic, arrogant selves!

Rather, on the other hand, even the vilest and wiliest of corrupt thrust a banknote into his palm, and the grumpiest of dames walking their dogs would place a packet of crackers beside his little knapsack, which had the happy smiley with the yellowish tinge as the logo!

The birds that nested on the lamppost, whose bulb had long since burned out, but wasn't replaced by the mayor's inspection team, also, as if in sympathy, would drop a few berries and other fruits to his feet. During the monsoon nights, he would be let into an old, disused outpost of the park guard by the sentry on duty. In summers, he would just lie back on the cobbled pavement and gaze long and hard at the stars in the blue sky overhead. During the winters, his old army coat served him well.

Nobody knew where he came from, and none dared speak to him for fear of being infected with his godforsaken fate of poverty, loneliness and wretched being! He never spoke to anybody either.

The years had gone by. Seasons had passed. His honesty was responsible for his early discharge from the armed forces department, in which he was in charge of stores & supplies of rations and arms to soldiers working on the frontiers of the land-locked country. He then set up a gas station in the veterans' quota, which too was grabbed by his civilian partners, by deceit. He had lost his ties with kith and kin, for he was one patriot that never availed himself of the leave facilities and did not attend his own wedding ceremony, nor visit his siblings and relatives. In time, he was disowned and assumed dead after a despatch wrongly listed him among the unfortunate soldiers who were attacked by enemy soldiers who violated a ceasefire, beheaded them and threw only their torsos onto this side of the border! The legal heir certificate was obtained, and a few vulture-like relatives had begun to draw his ex gratia monies. When he approached them back in the village, he was threatened with arrest for impersonation of a dead person! Dejected, he had utilised the last ounce of his energy to make a hasty retreat from there, take a train to this remote city and assume an identity which required no identity card, nor decorum and formalities in everyday life!

He was now 90 years of age, but a worry-free lifestyle, green environment and breaking free of all life's shackles seemed to add to his lifespan on earth. The sun and the moon were his parents, doting upon him by daybreak and nightfall. All the stars were his companions. Nature was his truest relative, not other human beings!

Poverty was a state of mind. Wealth was a way of life. Health was governed by degrees of stress in life. Wants are ghosts that haunt a cemetery! Food and air were always provided by an Almighty who blesses us with life and birth. Attractions are distractions. Breathe free. Be freed. Let go of artificial attachments. Illusions were allusions. Religion is a crutch with which the cowardly and the bravest alone tread in life's journey. Prayer is but a mindful wish. Procreation only adds to the train of miseries, struggles and vanity of mankind! Animals and birds are wiser than mankind. Is man not born alone to die alone?

Mercy, compassion, and kindness are present in every creation of God, a supreme Force of the Universe! Cruel twists and turns of fate are not lines which criss-cross on the palm of a hand, but the wavering mindsets of mankind which mislead with greed, envy, anger, selfishness, and a diffident nature being the strings that maul the heart!

Even as he was, for the first time in years, making these pronouncements to the rose bush that was springing up in the middle of the sidewalk, he breathed his last. A meteor came crashing down towards Earth. A thick fog enveloped the whole district the next morning. It was only after the annual snow clearance drive, announced by a political candidate for the local elections due after Christmas, that the body of Mr. Hope was discovered and laid to rest by another ex-army man, who spotted the tattoo of 'military intelligence' visible clearly on the right forearm of the unknown 'friendly, neighbourhood man', as the local news channel labelled him!

The knapsack with the happy yellow smiley was found to contain a manuscript called 'From Arms to Alms, Saga of Honesty!' This was published as a tribute to the demise of humanity among blood relations by the "mistress of spices', a wealthy woman who owned a house of disrepute: all proceeds were pledged to her charity that worked for "uplifting of plight of the down-trodden in a brutal society'.

Latest reports say the book grossed a record sum, outdoing pulp fiction on shades of emotions and fictional fairy tale characters, which had transformed the life of an unpublished authoress from forlorn & poor to celebrity of grandeur!

This, the power of the raw nature of endurance, evolution and endlessness of human travails in an enlightened, technology-driven life on the fast-lane!

9.

A lady bird!

She was the prettiest looking bird to whom the greenwood forest had ever been home. A new arrival as the bride of a big cat, she was adored by all the milder inhabitants, even as wild beastly ones cast an evil eye upon her. She, however, was innocent as ever. When the daisies danced to her cooing at dawn and dusk, the pretty young thing was reminded of her parental nest, down South in the hilly region, where all prevailed upon her to do the community song & dance show. Birds of all feathers would flock around the huge clearing atop the solitary guava fruit tree. She would spend hours hopping up the branches, daydreaming as all maidens of her age used to…!

Her parents had chosen this big cat as her spouse and, after a grand feast for all animals & birds of the neighbouring woods, left her in her husband's den, and returned to their own forest-city.

Time flew by. She brought two little birds into this world, and forgot the tortures meted out to her by her in-laws and husband by immersing herself in raising her bird-babies. The hay of her nest was often drenched by her tears, and it acted as her lone confidante.

More time passed by. One sunrise in autumn season, she was drawn to the verses of a human sage being played loudly on the forest guard's smartphone. Oh, those humans had a way with expression of feelings, and with communication. She made random queries and soon found herself perching atop a tall coconut tree, looking down at the saintly form seated in a posture of deep meditation.

Hours later, she saw him look up and smile benevolently. Responding to his gesture of welcome, she flew down to prostrate herself before the learned, wise man. Being a lady of virtuous disposition, she felt herself sobbing and bless-echoing the holy man to save her and her baby-birds from the awful torturous big cat, her spouse, and his wicked kith & kin.

She noticed the sage close his eyes for a few moments, apparently looking into her life's past, present, and future through his Third Eye. The serene soul then spoke in a quiet tone: "Yes. But the Lord who protects is greater than evil ones who wish to inflict injury. I will pray for your happy life, and that of your loved ones. But you must stop eating worm-food and mingling with wicked cats, hereafter. And sport a red spot of protection on your forehead. Do not let evil misguide you in the name of partying or such other forms of gallivanting."

He then pulled out an amulet from his right arm and asked the Lady Bird to don it around her neck but not let it be visible even to her big catty husband.

She accepted the protection-guard, bowed in reverence, and flew back to her nest-house!

Months turned into years. She adhered to the sage's advice obediently. Things had begun to change. Within a fortnight, she had been gifted a huge bird house of her own by her big cat and in-laws. Her catty sisters-in-law ceased to visit her place and turn her husband against her. Her baby birds' health improved, and they were faring well in their studies. She herself would wake up and say the prayer imparted to her by the sage.

Soon, her big cat of a husband brought in a wagon load of twelve pieces of jewellery, boasting of his intelligence and success. He sold off the items in the grey market to unsuspecting women-customers (wives of highly placed officials in government of human-beings) little informing the gullible purchasers that these were 'made in China' and not from 'Swiss banks', as he had announced to them!

The atmosphere was now wholly changed in the huge birdhouse. A home-theatre set, gymnastics equipment, fancy cars to ferry the grown-up bird kids and many more things that added to paraphernalia of wealthy human beings transformed the air. She too was corrupted by the relatives and opportunistic friends that began to frequent the bird-mansion. All these airs soon turned the grounded, docile Lady Bird into as monstrous a creature as her husband and in-laws.

She was soon convinced of her riches having come her way not due to the non-stop penance of that unsung sage in the jungle, through rain and shine, day and night, but wholly on account of her own destiny, smart spouse and lucky kids!

One night, she heard the voice of the sage in her sleep, cautioning her from succumbing to artificial, imaginary allurements, for evil was out to throttle her life, to bring in a harem of slave-wives.

She was also asked not to remove the sacred amulet under any circumstance.

The Lady Bird pooh-poohed the voice, but her inner sense prevented her from removing the amulet.

She, however, began a whispering campaign which spread throughout the greenwood forest and surrounding woods that the Sage was a fake beast, out to eat the birds, and that he must be shunned as a pariah would be by human beings in the society of gadgetry and sophistication. In this, she was aided by a few crows and cuckoos, as well as hyenas and other members of the forest club of ladies!

One said, "There is no God."
Another squeaked, "Holy men? As extinct as dinosaurs."

Yet another lady bird of high status said, "He can only be a man, not God!"

The chorus worked on her mind and, sipping her pomegranate juice, she deputed her servant, a jackass, to go out to the nearest forest settlement of human beings and spread malignant rumours about the sage, so that her newfound friends would remain pleased with her, and the secret of her re-birth, as the proverbial Phoenix emerged, would remain unknown to anybody. She smiled to herself ruefully, even as she began to sing her bird tunes merrily.

The sage, who was on non-stop fasting prayers for the poor, suffering bird, continued, though, to meditate on the ways of Nature; a huge amount of his physical energies were drained out by endowing the power of his spiritual grace to bestow peace, health & wealth on the hapless bird and her chicks. To what end? And at what cost?

Such is the prowess of compassion, mercy, suffering, evil, goodness, ingratitude, and wickedness; that each battle to outshine the other. Here comes the necessity for a religion, an order of faith and need to harbour a good conscience!

The Saga of the Lady Bird does not end, even when she turned against her protector based on hearsay and foul play of her big cat and minion companions. The Sage knows what is in store and continues to meditate for the bird who scorns her saviour. She was his adopted protegé. The Almighty had sent a suffering being to seek his help, and he had done the miracles of Almighty: the success of penance.

But his health deteriorates even as the Beneficiaries remain unaffected by the result of their inhuman attitudinal change. He shall live on, even without breathing, to pour life into a multitude of future generations as a Saint. But the hurt of being mistaken by his Beneficiaries singes his bright Soul.

Lady Bird is smarter than her big cat. She does not take off the sacred amulet, for she knows her big, fat cat would devour her and her baby-birds and wear the feathers around his neck, if ever she let the charm of divine-protection be separated from her bodily form!

A Lady Bird smiles on… The Sage meditates… The World cares less…

Rest in Peace!

10.

Garden of Stars

I know I am the lone witness to all the events on Earth, down below. My lord, the majestic Sun, would shine all day long, and I step in to rise high above the sea levels and watch the happenings of those that assume the Lord of the Universe is away and so they could indulge in whatever pastime they wish, beyond the sunset hours…

For some, these are happy hours. The tired workers rush home to relax with their beloved family. Most others, nowadays, believe in chasing away blues or cheering themselves with intoxicating substances – often drinks and merriment.

Many more dine on a fallen apple piece, or food left over by pot-bellied merchants, and then huddle beneath the railings of overpasses, flyovers and makeshift shelters. Some hid their forms under parked trucks, much like canines do for want of a shelter called home!

These humans had a very strange evolution from the pre-historic days of barbarism to the ingenious clan of life-forms that created a make-believe globe with artificial borders and fences guarded to prevent free movement, and yet issued visas to welcome those who spend man-made money and return to their respective homelands.

They failed to recognise that man was made to be different from the beasts and animals; the birds and the amphibians; the plants and the womenfolk on earth! They knew, over the course of evolution of civilisation, that the blood and body parts, as well as functions of these, were identical amongst them all. They knew that they all were born and that eventually all died. But they spread out across topographical zones and developed distinct senses of culture, tradition, flags, songs, dances, dietary and culinary habits, and even a babel of tongues!

In the recent century, mankind had established a United Nations organisation, and even began to be knit into one web-world entwined by Internet technology, as they termed it, but still thrived on comparative analyses, differential pricing regimes and unequal currency measurements as a yardstick of their progress and dominance over one another! Societal mores changed rapidly, and the unthinkable judicial acceptance of such hitherto frowned upon practices added pace to the unnatural transformation of that bluish mass of floating body called Earth, around which I am assigned to rotate on my axis!

Well, the nocturnal creatures such as the owl and prowling wild animals in search of prey for food and survival kept me company. As I noticed to my astonishment, mankind too had its set of burglars and leech-like criminals that step out under the cover of

darkness to steal, usurp, and injure others with selfish motives…
And then there was the ever increasing trend of smoky jet machines which criss-crossed the cloudy skies, closely followed by man-made satellites that beamed data for not-always-holy purposes to their master computers and programmes, way down in sealed corridors of power and wealth, covered by the umbrella and seal of governance of fellow-beings!

All the other stars, even the constellations, were disgusted and dismayed by the poor visibility of things on the watery planet Earth, and thus it was left upon only myself, as the Lord's Consort, to attend to all those that looked up at the sky with a prayer on their lips or seeking succour from Heaven above their little selves!

I give you the introduction above only to highlight the great spectacles I do get to watch from my exalted position in the night skies! For one, none of those floodlights, neon lamps or the solar powered mass lighting can ever match up to the cool beauty of my beams. The cruellest of men as well as the loveliest of women are but influenced by the degree and extent of my beams touching them as they grew within the confines of the mother's womb – a cosmic secret little known to the best of super-computers!

Thus, it was only my radiance and charm which could rectify characters or nurture goodwill among these creatures whom the Almighty created supposedly in His Form: little wonder also then that so-called rational thinking people pooh-poohed the existence of a God or that gods & goddesses did indeed resemble their beings and forms.

From time to time and across the eons, I do rise to the call of Destiny and direct the celestial power of my moonbeams towards a chosen couple to get them to fall madly, passionately in love and depict a tale or saga of loyalty and worship of love, while being born as humans and leading a life on earth! This is essential to restore the semblance of sanity and humanity among mankind: when Divinity is at play, to what end are the deceit and evil perpetrated by mankind's own ilk?

Here is one such instance of my intervention to transform cold blooded, warring earthlings into the humane, loving persona of the Unseen Force – Almighty God!

It was early dawn and about 4 a.m. Earth time! A 'guru' – one who guides another from darkness of ignorance towards the light of wisdom by gifting the lamp of knowledge – was preaching to his group of disciples in that blessed portion of Earth known through the ages as 'Bharat' and crowned by the ageless Himalayas. He suddenly asked if anyone present there was capable of raising a garden of flowers in that region, braving the cold climate, the ubiquitous mosquitoes, the insects, rodents, and reptiles in order to present the flowers to the Deity of the Almighty who presided atop the seven hills. The Lord loved to be adorned in flowers, he pointed out.

One among the group of disciples raised his hand, stood up, bowed in reverence, and submitted his desire to take up the task. Prostrating in the traditional way, he sought the blessings of his Revered Guru and, after sunset, set out with his wife to find a large tract of land in the Tirumala hills. Soon, he prepared a flower garden and began to send the flowers for garlands to be prepared and hung around the neck of the presiding deity. However, he thirsted for more to be done in the service of the Lord.

He wanted to send flowers that were even more beautiful and fragrant. He wanted to raise a garden around the temple for this purpose. To begin with, he wanted to dig a tank for supply of water to the garden itself; hence he took the assistance of his spouse and began to dig the water-tank. Since he was the main priest offering worship during the daytime in the temple, he and his wife would begin to dig the trench, and gradually build the tank itself, after sunset hours. I, the moon, was their companion, shining within them as their 'Faith'...

As a few days passed by like this, The Lord was touched by the dedication, devotion and sincerity of the couple. He walked up to the man in the form of a young lad and offered to help, but was denied permission by the man, who said that it was a sin to extract laborious tasks from minors and little children, especially since he had no money to pay wages for such labour. This sense of justice and compassion only impressed The Lord further and he firmly resolved to Grace his devotee. God always is more determined to bestow his Grace upon His Devotees for the faithfulness exhibited by them.

The husband would dig with a crowbar whilst his wife would carry the soil in a basket to a far corner of the land and dump it there, despite being at an advanced stage of pregnancy!

Now, The Lord assumed the form of a young child and approached the woman and pleaded to assist her in the task: the lady could not refuse the wish of a child who seemed to enjoy it! Thus, it came to pass that no sooner would the man dig out a heap of soil and put it in the basket would the woman go and return seemingly in no time and without any signs of exertion even in her physical state of carrying a to-be-born baby in her womb!

Unable to hide his curiosity, he asked her the secret of her energy! The lady declared that she was being helped by a sweet looking child. This infuriated her husband because he disliked taking help from others! He ambled quickly across the tract of land and chased the boy, who only ran around playfully in circles and giggled. It seemed a hide-and-seek game, almost akin to the game which clouds play with me, the moon, or the sea waves! But the short-tempered devotee was livid with rage and, looking up towards me shining bright up above, as a full moon at the midnight-hour, he hurled the crowbar at the little boy: the flying missile glinted in the moonbeams that tried to shroud The Lord in his hour of crisis, but it hit the boy's chin. Being in a human form, the wound began to bleed profusely, and he disappeared among the flowers of the garden and retired to his Sanctum Sanctorum of the Temple. After a few minutes of searching for the naughty lad, the man resumed digging the land, in a bid to build the water-tank!

At the break of dawn, he bathed and, applying sandalwood paste to his forehead, he stepped into the temple, only to find a huge commotion in there! The Lord had a bleeding wound on his chin and the efforts of his fellow priests to press camphor and turmeric against it appeared futile; the blood kept dripping from the Deity sculpted of dark granite stone!

As a moonbeam touched his forehead through the temple tower's intricate arch designs, the truth dawned on him and the ardent devotee began to sob and prostrated himself before the Almighty Lord with folded hands and a repentant heart, sobbing uncontrollably. He begged to be forgiven. He was blinded by a magnificent obsession to dig the water tank and grow a beautiful garden of flowers to be offered to The Lord he worshipped, but failed to recognise the fact that His Lord was gracing him with personal assistance and had, as a result, acted in a hasty, foolish manner, inflicting an injury on the very God he worshipped for protection and good health!

The Almighty Lord, then stepping out of the sculpted form, embraced the man and declared that the camphor on the chin will forever be a reminder to the world at large of the greatest devotion exhibited by this devotee, who grew the rarest of rare flowers to be adorned in the course of worship of the Divine!

This incident I witnessed occurred circa 1113 CE of the modern-day Gregorian calendar!

Now, as I shine on that region atop the seven hills, which has grown enormously in pilgrimage popularity and tourist traffic, I still find that the garden is filled with trees of several hues and fragrances: I alone know that to this date, The Lord and His Consort walk into this garden and, finding the flowers magnificent, pluck and smell them, and as they throw them into the air, these turn into stars in the heavens above earth and throw their radiance upon every being born on the hour of their own transformation into stars! The crowbar with which 'the star gardener' inflicted the injury on The Lord is displayed to this day, in circa 2023 CE, and whoever visits the magnificent Tirumala Temple of Lord Venkataramana would see this testimony of devotion, love and grace hanging prominently both on entry as well as exiting from the main entrance!

Spiritual religions believe in the power of flowers, and if adorned as a garland to a deity of worship, absolute protection from all evil and negative forces of Nature is assured by cosmic power and the Grace of the Almighty!

I, the fair and lovely moon you all so adore, would leave you to muse and contemplate on the fact that the author I am using to pen this account of the 'garden of stars' also has a childhood cut below the chin and can see souls, not forms in human beings and other creatures of life! And I am his muse, of course!

Food for thought?

11.

The Star-Mantra

He was an avid star gazer from childhood. The science teacher at primary school, as well as his parents, had instilled in him the love for the dazzling night skies, so much so that even during monsoon season, he would often peer through the dark cloudy sky to espy a star or two winking at him, faintly or bright…and the determined gazer would smile with joy, wave a hand, make a wish and retire into his homestead to dream on… His grandmother, who first narrated a fairy tale at bedtime, taught him to make a wish whenever he noticed a falling star shooting down from the sky, or a cluster of these mysterious cosmic beings dancing in a circle!

And he took pride in passing the science and pleasure of this art of sky watching and stargazing to his children, and now, it was the turn of his youngest grandchild, a blue eyed, freckled three-year-old girl ambling along by his side as he clutched a walking stick and treaded the way up the hill on a bright starry night in the Himalayan village.

Even the full moon, who was shining in full glow, could not but help admire this beautiful pair of humans. She sent a moonbeam straight at them.

As they reached the clearing atop the hill, he sat down on the green grass and his little granddaughter did likewise. He told the child to lie back and look up at the sky. It was a wide-angled view, he told her. From this spot, one could view as much as almost three fourths of the Earth's sky, it seemed! He soon began to teach her, in a subtle manner, of the existence of stars, constellations, satellites, planets, solar systems, galaxies and the pole star. Her grandpa then told her of how the three wise men, the Magi, followed the star in the desert land to reach a stable; he also told her about zodiac signs and the Arundati star... He spent a great deal of the pleasant evening and night, well past dinner time, explaining to the little child how important it is to be aligned to Mother Nature in life.

She also got inducted into learning the morals of a humanitarian society and the egalitarian principles that moulded life on earth. In the course of the next five years, she was able to astound her science teachers with the fount of knowledge she exhibited in astronomy and moral science class tests.

Her mentor and beloved grandfather left for the heavenly abode when she turned eighteen. He was believed to be a hundred and eight years old! A ripe old age, they said. But she knew that he lived on through her and her siblings too; knowledge passed on from generation to generation helped evolve mankind, but also held civilisation firmly on place! Personal values alone helped shape the destiny of a person, she believed. She pooh-poohed the concepts of 'fate', 'luck' and 'karma' doled out by her peers at college. Well, as life shaped up, she won a scholarship to the foremost space university in the United States of America, and, before long, was selected to be an astronaut on an international space mission.

As the D-day for take-off drew nearer, she felt a sense of serenity overtake her, even as her colleagues were perceptibly anxious. She carried a little idol of the Hindu God of Success, Vighneswara, that her grandfather had presented to her as a reward on her topping a national science quiz for the first time at age five! The tiny God was her lucky mascot, whom she desired to take along into space!

She was seated in the commander's seat at the front of the space-ship as she noticed that, in the vacuum of space on earthly day number three, a battery of a dozen oval-shaped vessels was tailing the craft! Ground mission control could not see these followers on the radar and computer screens, they muttered loud and clear from the overhead speakers fitted to her armchair styled seat. She did not let fear creep into her mind though. She was a positive-minded person, and by virtue of her beloved grandpa's training, could recite ancient verses of Indian scriptures which were said to help communicate with the air, water, fire, energy, and space sorrow during life on earth. He had also blessed her with the secret knowledge of an unheard-of mantra, which, when prayed in a deep breath could help break the shackles of time warp and enable intergalactic communication, as well as journeys between eras, old, recent and future! She was told to invoke it only in outer space and when in a state of deep crisis!

The prayer was with her every living moment on Earth but out here and now, when she was in real need of it, the mantra appeared to elude her memory.

The next she knew, she found herself in alien territory, seated on a throne embedded with what she felt were dazzling bright stars, the orbs of light she had raved about all through her childhood. The atmosphere itself was earthen and peaceful, with a soothing waterfall playing a hitherto unheard piece of instrumental music. To her right was a lovely being; she presumed it was a female of the species, because she was adorned in pink attire and almost a million gemstones and scented flower robes dangled beside her form. And to her left was a being even the best of make-up artists or graphic designers on earth could not chisel – Adonis, Eros, and Bond would all seem ugly ducklings before this Emperor, she thought, in bewilderment.

"You are in Utopia, the land which Homer, your grandfather's buddy, wrote about! We welcome you to our universe! But pray tell us where to find the secret 'map of love' on earth! You are brought here only to learn this knowledge from your being and escort you back to that little toy craft of yours!"

She was amazed!

Yes, indeed, her grandpa had discussed the 'map of love'! How spine chilling to imagine that one would be captured in outer space by aliens to discover one of the most safely guarded Earth secrets! The secret of life on Earth!

She for one knew that it wasn't a nuclear formula of Einstein, or Aryabhata's mathematical magic. A mantra could pour life, save lives or avert a catastrophe on Earth, if uttered in the right manner by a righteous soul at an opportune time! But why would Utopians vie for such an ancient Earthly secret of life?

As though reading her thoughts, the Queen smiled. "The knowledge of the map of love was imparted to you when the Moonbeam bathed you on that summer's night in your Himalayan village, sweetheart! Recall the mantra your elder taught you dear one! We will set you back on your journey with gratitude!"

Try as she might, the Star Gazer astronaut-woman could not rec-ollect the magic mantra!

"Recall your lifetime since childhood on the lap of your elders, my child!" rang the sing-song voice of that handsome Emperor.

Exotic looking fruits were placed on a huge platter made appar-ently of emerald rocks (or chunks of kryptonite, she mused) be-fore her. As she suddenly felt ravenously hungry, she descended on an apple-like fruit and a whole bunch of orange grape fruits! Nectar like syrup was offered to drink down the food.

"Ahh…!"
This was from a new entrant to the hall … Lo and behold!
This being resembled her beloved grandfather, who had indoc-trinated her to the world of the stars and sky as a toddler!

Oh, my goodness! But it cannot be! She struggled with logic and emotions bordering love, surprise and joy – all mixed into one gushing moment of unspeakable happiness! She broke down into tears and wept for almost an Earth day!

But she was transfixed to his gaze, and neither the apparition of her grandpa nor she could step an inch! It was as though a video conferencing session was on!

And then she noticed tears trickling down her grandpa's look-alike figure, which spoke aloud, "Sweetu, do recite the mag-ic mantra and translate its meaning to these good Samaritans of Space-world… Only then will my soul rest in peace as well as their clan live on in harmony. Presently, they have a vacuum filled essence with only plentiful prosperity and no challenges to look forward to in daily existence – it is all humdrum and the monotony is inflicting pain upon them all!"

The mantra sprang out of her mouth!

At once, the Utopian Emperor and his Consort rose out of their thrones and seemed to glide to her seat in a fraction of a second. 'In a Blink!'

"… Oh, we know this is the simplest translation of your ancient world mantra, but please enlighten us in layman terms of you Earthlings!'

She smiled now in full confidence gained from the startled expressions and naive request received. "'I love you!': when translated into intergalactic English language, this mantra simply means these three words … It is the map of love by which hearts beat on; minds race on; mankind lives on earth through eras, ages and leap years! An expression well used by a mother or father to their child or by siblings to one another or between lovers and strangers; this may be reflected in a gesture as a handshake, a hug, a gentle nudge, offering food to the hungry; shelter to the homeless; blankets to those shivering on an old wintry night; or showing mercy, compassion, kindness, and sharing joy by breaking bread or clinking glasses of milk or wine whilst in company of other fellow human beings! …Such is the map of love which sustains mankind's survival on Earth, through earthquakes, tsunamis, typhoons, cyclones, famine, drought, or even man-made disasters like wars and boundaries for sharing the oil, water, gas, food and air – all nature's resources, over which mankind has no proprietary claim, whatsoever!

"So, even when under attack by other men, there exists a bonhomie, and among others similarly placed, and those wronged, love flows. This milk of love alone helps refugees, oppressed and hapless weaker beings, survive to live on, and the power of resilience is nothing but the power of love!

"… It is not natural calamities; it is definitely not man-made catastrophes; but the spread of love among individuals in times of difficulty as well as peace is responsible for the survival of harmony over angst and hatred!"

A warm hand clasp by the Emperor and his better-half sent a surge of energy through her, the like of which the astronaut hadn't ever read about, even in science fiction thrillers or scriptures of different faiths which existed on earth, her home-planet!

As she opened her eyes, she found herself being surrounded by a bevy of press reporters and television channel reps posing a single, common question to her:

"Ma'am, Commander, could you explain the insignia 'In A Blink' engraved in gold and studded with rare, previously unseen gemstones that has appeared on the top of your spacecraft?"

The beaming Earth woman replied with a smile and, pointing towards the little idol in white marble she held in her hand, mumbled – "Map of Love!

"Oh, that's code for 'I love you'!"

A thunderous applause drowned the rest of her explanation. . .

12.

A Star-Child!

June was a sweet looking young girl, aged seven, whose twinkling eyes and bright smile won her several fans amongst her family's friends, as well as her teachers and the parents who visited her day school. Her father was a high-ranking official in the State Government, and always had escort vehicles filled with security guards who toted guns and batons, called 'lathis' in the local language. Her mother was pretty as a rose, but she was always occupied with her busy schedule of kitty parties and ladies' club events. Little June soon began to grasp that mommy was for goodnight kisses and good morning blushes, while Daddy was like God himself to his followers, and like good old Santa Claus, who visited only once a year with goodies for her, in particular. She had a train of attendants led by the governess, Sonia.

June soon began to develop an interest in crayons and colours. She began to paint the sun, the moon, the trees, the birds, the riverside, the mountains and even the host of gods and goddesses her friend Shilpi at school showed her upon one of the rare visits to her farm house, and which her mother, Rosemary, told her were all imaginary and non-existent. But the curiosity of the child got the better of her.

June soon began to learn the finer aspects of the elephant-headed Ganesha as well as the monkey-god, Anjaneya, or Hanuman, alongside the man-lion form of Lord Narasimhaswami, from her maid servant, the ever-sporting jasmine flowers Malathi, who also wore a round vermillion mark on her forehead.

June began to ponder on why a few of her friends at school were worshipping various parts of Nature, while one particular teacher at school always donned a veil on her way to school, but magically wore western attire upon reaching the school premises. Who is God? What differentiates one human being from another? Why are some against the freedom of others? Why are some flowers of the same shape and colour, whereas some others take different colours but are of the same shape? Why does the sun set here in the evenings, while it then rises in America, where her favourite aunt, Julie, lives? Why must she stay awake a few hours or arise in the middle of her sleep to answer Auntie Julie's sweet questions?

June liked Christmas the best of all days in the year: her school was closed for the winter vacation. Her father was home and so was her mommy. All the cousins, uncles and aunts gathered in her house. There was warmth and bonhomie all around the huge private estate.

She was the darling of all and the apple of her parents' eyes. All the affection helped her carry through the rest of the twelve months!

June learnt not to shed tears in presence of others, but the huge teddy bear she hugged to sleep was a witness to the pails and wells filled with the her tears. She was a sensitive child, but very sensible too. Her delicate mind hurt on seeing the acts of discrimination and differentiation her otherwise loving parents meted out to a few servants and employees in the sprawling office behind the family church at the rear of the compound.

June was determined to play Santa Claus this December 25th. She drew up a list of all her poorer friends at school, and the lame and maimed ones in the retinue of her father's servants. Sonia, the elderly governess, truly liked this little mistress and supported her in the Christian adventure. Little presents were gathered out of the handsome pocket money allocated to June each month by her father. Both painstakingly wrapped them, and the angelic little girl even scrawled her wishes against each name of every packet.

Hiding them was not difficult, because nobody stepped into her room outside of the fixed visits by her parents or Malathi.

June, however, fell ill all of a sudden as the grand occasion neared, and was rushed to a nursing home. Her daddy was away in China and Mommy was at a social service event, leading a candlelit march in the national capital for some unfortunate girl who was assaulted brutally by drunken lorry drivers while hitching a lift at night on a remote stretch of the town. Sonia and other members of the housekeeping staff rushed the child to the nearest nursing home.

June was suffering from pneumonia, the doctors diagnosed. All required treatment was being administered to the pretty child. However, as the head nurse, an ex-nun, commented, "This child is pining for the love of her parents, not for medicines; she is not sick, but ill, and she must be sent home and asked to be tended by her parents, not by unknown doctors in a strange building!"

June was visibly unwell and as the child's face turned pale, Sonia was in tears; Malathi was on an indefinite fasting prayer and was visiting all the temples that dotted the region, seeking divine intervention and grace of the Almighty who she, like her ilk, believed manifests in various forms of Mother Nature.

June would whisper out to them asking how many days were now left for Father Christmas, Santa Claus to make his appearance. Initially, the doting staff mistook it for a yearning for gifts and arranged for a tiny Christmas tree to be placed in her room by the bedside to cheer her up, and with a commercial view to charge her very wealthy father a few extra bucks for value added services. But that did not cheer the sweet little patient nor halt her question – "How many days more for Santa Claus to come?"

June was sinking, despite the best medical attention, and Christmas Day just a week away. Sonia spoke at length to her mistress, Madam Rosemary, who said the March was a great success and hogged media attention, and so she had to do the rounds of television studios for interviews and could not afford to break her commitments to society. Her husband was leading a delegation to China and had public interest in mind as well. So, it was Sonia's duty to attend to her ward, and she would get a raise in salary for the trouble. Aghast, the old governess kept staring at the mobile phone in her clenched fist and broke into helpless tears at the shame and irony of it all!

June developed a complicated condition which prompted the attending physicians to put her on a heavy dosage of sleeping pills. Malathi and Sonia faithfully tended to the little darling girl and prayed for deliverance. Malathi was prepared to see her daughter or herself suffer the feverish pain in place of June, such was her new prayer. Sonia begged of the Almighty Lord to cure the child at once. The head nurse would still grumble that she was an Angel who sought compassion, love, and harmony and not deliverance from pain or suffering!

June was sinking as December 24th arrived, and so did her folks, followed by the whole army of relatives, friends and associates of her father. All flocked to see the frail baby girl, whose face lit up on seeing her near and dear ones, especially her beloved parents. Sonia was permitted to stand by the bedside, but poor Malathi, of a different religion, was sent out of the nursing home to return home and do the chores of serving the guests.

June saw her Mommy dumping huge gift-wrapped items beside her, and her father sitting grimly in a chair lost in deep thought. Both seemed lost to the world, and all of a sudden, she was inspired by a thought.

June beckoned her father to her and as the stern-faced powerful man walked to her with a smile, the daughter told him that she had a secret to tell him: only asking for him to stay and all others to leave the room for a while. "Mommy must go too, please!"

June heard her father bark out an order and both father and child were left alone for what seemed only half an hour to those waiting outside, but these few minutes were more than enough for the little daughter to ask her father to narrate the story of the birth of the good shepherd, and the importance of familial values over street marches and huge business empires or political seats of power over the rest of the world.

June saw her strong, brave, tough father break down in tears, and she was hugging him as though their roles were transformed by an unseen Force, and he was the child and she his elder!

June read in the next day's papers of how everyone was stunned as her Father convened a hurried press conference to announce his retirement from business, politics and public life. He and his wife had a job to do: first and foremost, to set their house in order and watch the growing up of their little daughter, who was battling for life alone. Christian values sought to show how charity begins from home and how much more valuable it is for a man to be a good husband, a loving father and a responsible house-holder than some face in the crowd that leads a mob to some goal imagined by many unknowns!

June learnt that her father then arranged for a get together of all the beneficiaries of her Surprise Christmas presents, and she miraculously leapt out of her bed in the Hospital and asked to be taken home. The chirpy child was back, and Sonia and the head nurse exchanged knowing glances. The Lord of All touched her father through her loving being!

June, to this day, celebrates Christmas with her dear parents, as well as her doting husband and children and the bevy of servants and other relatives who did not vanish with the voluntary renunciation of power and wealth by her dear Father.

Santa Claus too makes it a point to visit all those other masses of humanity across the world, who see him through different lenses, calling those other occasions Deepavali, Dussehra, Pongal, Bihu, Sankranti, Holi and Ramadan!

Merry Christmas in December and a happy Christmas to those celebrating Life and the joys of being together in June, July, August and every other month of the Gregorian calendar!

June urges one and all to share the happiness of being a Family and shun the far away riches to the wealth of togetherness, peace and harmony throughout life.

Merry Christmas All...

13.

Soul of Love!

There was no respite from the wildfires. It was the strangest season the nine-hundred-year-old grand tree had witnessed. The last was a couple of centuries ago, when a part of his vast branches was engulfed for a few hours and the ashen portion of his majestic form was splashed all across the national newspapers with the banner, "World's oldest banyan tree charred in wildfire but escapes a glorious ending!" Ugh …! Even to think of how inhuman a few of these humans can be sent shudders all across his veins, branches and deeply rooted self.

This time around, the television channels were agog with stunning, breaking-news tales of human loss and a gross failure to comprehend the vagaries of Nature. Mankind did progress across the medieval times through the industrial revolution to the even more dramatic computer technological era, which totally upheaved the lifestyles, thought processes and pace of life across the planet. More and more folk began to envision themselves as demigods, and a vast number of them played devils: nay, hacking was not a wrong, per se, as there was 'ethical' hacking and vicious hacking, mused the grand old Tree... There were satellites orbiting the space up above which spied on happenings down below – the weathermen down below, in air-conditioned cubicles, analysed the stream of data and forewarned Earthlings! Such was the way man depended upon gadgetry, digital and mechanical, for every walk of life nowadays, especially in the post-IT era, so much so that even those who ruled nations communicated with their citizenry via video screens, Internet messages and propagandists! No more did the ruler go incognito and throw blankets over the homeless that sleep crouched under the shade of trees, or distribute fruits and bread to the hungry, helpless, lame and maimed, less fortunate people in the country! No more did a wise minister preside over the cabinet of the king, but a lobbyist firm or survey group backed by nongovernmental bodies fomented policies and led revolutions; signature campaigns online determined the popularity, and voting was reduced to a farcical exercise where pollsters became soothsayers of the mind of the public at large.

Such were the times when peace was much in demand, as well as the scarcest commodity in a world immersed in consumerism and lethargy. Purchases were made online and picnics no longer meant walking along with the family (children included) to the shade of the trees on the mountain top or by the lakeside, but ambling into large concrete jungles called 'shopping malls', and desert lands had 'ice skating rinks' whilst colder regions had dry 'race tracks' which substituted for Nature.

Was it human nature which had been transformed by the ingenuity of mankind, or is it Nature's ingenuousness which had led to a stage of human beings cloning, experimenting and meddling with Mother Nature to mess up the climatological calculations of Nature and result in such misfortunes?

As the grand old banyan tree pondered, it also occurred to him that he would be dubbed an 'ancient' by these upstarts, who dreamt of tossing out old world values and trading the soul for sole proprietorship of immortality!

I happened to be the little bird whose nest rested nestling in the lovely, cool branches of this magnificent witness to the history of mankind! You would be glad to know that all my forefathers also had their nests atop this noble creation of Almighty Nature: I lose count of the several generations who benefitted from the presence of this mighty, compassionate tree sheltering a variety of creatures. The lush green valley is the garden of paradise because of this mighty soul labelled the 'banyan tree' by intelligent humans! Why cannot you human beings be human? To be human is not to unravel mysteries unknown to mankind, but to pour life, treasure lives and stay immortal by acts of compassion (not passion), deeds of kindness (not arrogance), and breathe love (not hatred)… Lest you be exterminated as a race, please bring home the birds to nestle in the nests of Nature: do not pollute natural traits, habitats and climates!

May Man again begin to live to be a thousand years old as he did in eras gone by!

May better sense prevail so the wildness of Man shall not douse the fire of the spirit of mankind but ignite the soul of love!

May each man be the Banyan tree – so that no brushfire can prove him a burnout in the world!

14

Lady of Letters!

Mariana was proud to be a teacher. She had nurtured this ambition ever since she was at play school and watched how all the mothers who accompanied their little ones to school always bowed in deference and encouraged their children to present roses on almost every other day. The little child in her developed a keen sense of observation, and as she grew up, her penchant for discipline, as well as creativity, sharpened. She always topped the class and soon she graduated to become a high school teacher at the capital city's oldest school. But soon, the young teacher submitted her resignation to a promising career and returned to her village, located in the remotest corner of her country, and took up the position as the head mistress of her old play school.

Mariana relished every single moment of her time spent at the school. She indulged herself in the demands of her calling most religiously, and devoted full attention to each of her forty-five wards in all the five sections of the school, whom she was responsible to teach the basics of education. With her very elegant face forever poised high up in the air, like a proud peacock strutting her feathers, the 'lady of letters', as she came to be popularly known around the countryside, soon became so obsessed with her passion for imparting knowledge that she remained a spinster. The passing years had not left a trace on her zeal and the teacher in her soon took charge of all the other pupils of the surrounding schools on weekends to teach them skills in fine arts, debating, sports and such other extra-curricular activities.

Time, however, waits for no man, nor woman!

Society around her began to transform. Technological revolution happened. The net result was that traditional forms of imparting teaching to the children began to be considered obsolete by policy makers in the governments of the world. Nursery kids began to carry and indulge in appliances and gadgets, with which they played 'war games' and such other fiery video games, and virtual fun soon overtook the arena of learning.

Mariana felt lost, and continued to innovate the lessons to suit these 'modern mindsets', but the parents, as well as the students, were reluctant and recalcitrant about her coaxing them to 'not lose track of the roots of education'… She was demoted by the management, based on complaints received about her outdated methodology and moral lessons in a modern society.

Her love for teaching did not permit her to see sense, so to speak. She continued doting on her pupils. She still would go about instructing them in abacus, atlas, picture charts, crayons and chart paper craft works, but the newer breed seemed to be born with a yen for technology – tablets, iPads, iPods and the like – rather than to bend down and draw figures and practice handwriting exercises.

"Oh, good Lord!" she would exclaim under her breath.

She chanced to watch a newscast on television where the dynamic head of state was calling upon his countrymen to assess and determine the causes of children of immigrants performing much better than native children in academics. The answers were known to her, and she shot off a long letter of appreciation, filled with recommendations. The fate of her missive was not known to her, but she came to accept an overseas deputation in a less advanced country to teach the children there.

Mariana set out with trepidation at the unknown culture, but soon mingled with locals and became a hot favourite among the parents as well as the children who were taught under her leadership. A year of four seasons for the world outside, but she knew that for her it was a daily war, conquered because every titbit of learning helped churn out the best of pupils, and these studious children outshone their competitors. A matter of pride indeed for all concerned!

Mariana however was in for a rude shock when she watched another television newscast one fine morning in this land of envy for many others abroad: the government in power had decided to call off the examination system and allot grades to all children! What an ill-conceived move on part of the local minister for education, she muttered angrily. What is the world coming to? On her side of the planet were little kids toting their gadgets and neglecting the basic tools of education, and on this less-developed side of the world, with more industrious peoples, was the self-destructive move to abandon the system of instilling the spirit of competitiveness and turning everyone into an 'also-ran'! One rotten apple can spoil the whole basket, they say, but who is aping whom, and what is the cause of such foolhardy measures in an otherwise enlightened era?

Mariana returned to her homeland, disillusioned but with hope afresh. She was appointed the head of all institutions run by the same management as her primary school. She was even given a civic reception of honour by the local Sheriff. Yet she discovered in the space of a month that all she did nowadays was to sit in a solitary cabin before a giant screen and type orders, questions and answers mechanically, not knowing the faces of the recipients of her body of knowledge nor the expressions which shed light upon the I.Q. Levels or core abilities and capacities of each one of these future citizens of the world!

Mariana, the lady of letters, was drowned in a stream of tears – not of self-pity, but at the abject poverty of minds that governed the future, at present!

Are you but a drop of her tears or a gem of her world of words?

Let us all strive for a 100 per cent literate world, not a world which forgets the art and skills of education!

15.

Princess of Stars

She was the Princess of the Universe. Her bubbly presence was the joy of Father Time and pride of her mirror. When she smiled, the moonbeams spread far and wide, to the deepest ravines on planet Earth. As she burst into peals of laughter, little lighthouses sprang forth and occupied deep space as Stars that twinkled forever, and gleamed as lovingly at darkness so that all those other orbiting bodies of mass felt wanted, guarded, and would come alive, carrying life of various forms – humans, plants, animals and even a few stones called precious diamonds, rubies, and emeralds. But planet Earth was her favourite.

Legend has it that her home of Heaven was originally on Earth, but due to falling societal values across ages, her dear parents had to shift out and return back to abide above the 21st dimension of 'space'!

Barbaric practices, lawlessness, strife, and animosities appeared to govern the planet Earth. Inhumane laws and a failure to respect time-tested traditions resulted in unnatural practices bordering on edge of decadence as well as an extermination of human civilisation itself... So much so that the existence of the mighty Gods itself came to be questioned as an antiquated, superstitious belief of the learned, the old and the senile ones!

She, however, was the cynosure of all universe and determined to help restore serenity on Earth, the lone surviving celestial body in space. Mankind had embarked on sojourns in a scientific temper, and in tinkering with technological experimentation, had exploded nuclear material on Alien bodies, thereby destroying unique life-matter present upon each and every one of those other planets, exoplanets as well as their satellite-bodies.

Gods were real. Heaven was here. But her heart was on Earth. The Spirits had danced in joy when she was born! All space suddenly turned luminous again, and Solace woke up from a deep slumber to descend down on Earth. The foreboding of the astrologers and almanac-pundits was becoming reality. Those ancient sages, seated in deep penance over centuries, began to stir in the Himalayas. The atmosphere was new now: tall trees, little shrubs and glades in the valleys were swaying as if in song and their chorus affected the vibrations across glasshouses, and framed steel-clothing donned by a pollution-hit Earthling community. Hope leapt out of the forlorn world of drone-like robotic-mankind. Something was going to happen. Change was in the air. For the better, they all knew...!

***

He was still seated in the dense thick forest of tall, old green trees which seemed to dwarf the great Himalayas, which had been his abode for decades. The high, lofty peaks were snow-clad during winter and sprung to a magical new life after every such sheet of white icicles. He was immune to heat and dust, cold or warmth. He had a flowing beard, which he let remain as a stark reminder of the age on Earth. Before he had set out on a self-imposed exile from strands of modern civilisation, he was a fiery, spirited fighter of rights, reason, and knowledge. He was born and brought up into a culture of honesty, sincerity, sacrifice, compassion, kindness, and trust as a way of life. He soon stepped into the society of men and matters, distanced himself from alien women on a staunch belief of a destined better-half walking into his life at an opportune time. In the next three decades, he faced many a silent, lonely battle against the envious evil ones that could not digest his success in endeavour after endeavour. But, he soon found opportunism and hypocrisy ruling all across the haloed pillars of mankind, and as he was on the verge of being sworn in the head of an important State, he submitted his letter of refusal and, with folded hands, bowed out of limelight. That the mainstream media dubbed him variously as a coward, neo-Buddha and a flop in life only helped him seek oblivion. Very soon, he fell out of public memory, and even the odd call or two from relatives stopped soon, as the telecom network stopped functioning for lack of towers beyond the foothills of the green peak which offered him sanctuary, at over 5000 feet above sea level.

He began his penance, and in such a state of meditation, he was able to remotely control the governments of his motherland as well as other foreign lands, where people in general clamoured for peace and a hunger-free, law-abiding civilised existence. As is their wont, little minds that donned high offices around the globe claimed credit for the sudden fall in crime rates, famines, ravages of cyclones; for climate control, food control, gun control, wars being ended and a new sense of universal love settling over valleys, hamlets, societies... Cases of marital discord, domestic violence, child abuse, racism, apartheid, casteism, discrimination and ostracisation ended in no time, as it appeared to chroniclers of history. Even tarot-readers, astrologers, arms-dealers, drug-peddlers, racketeers, Mafia and cartels seemed to be as distant in time as the long-extinct dinosaurs; people found coexistence, community prayers and walking in the gardens or singing aloud tunes of one's own making a common joyous pastime. Hospitals were as crèches; no more hospices or hotbeds of corruption. Lawyers and psychiatrists were a tribe which sought newer vocations such as acting as tour-guides or social service para-legal personnel helping the militaries, who were engaged more in socially useful productive works, such as the construction of bridges linking all the seven continents of planet Earth. Flowers of new shades and varieties seemed to bloom all of a sudden. Birds were chirruping happily in abandon once again, as in the pre-Twitter era.

The swans and deer, as well as the peacocks and genteel cows, appeared to have increased in population as if they were rabbits and men. Literature was being retrieved from the deepest cellars of historical museums and cloud-space mode to which they were relegated, despite centuries of evolution. All in all, a universal world of free travel, abundant supply of food and all other resources needed to ensure that no man or animal died of hunger, want of scarcity. Utopia was an invented; a small word to describe this marvellous state of human life on Earth!

***

As and when there is a sincere prayer made on Earth, the Princess of Stars smiles to let a star slip down into the bowl of plenty which her betrothed, meditating since ages in the Himalayan forest ranges, has been utilising to fulfil the needs of the hungry, thirsty, sad, deprived and needy around the globe. The star would, upon contact with his palms, turn into a bright light and float through the environment to create happy climate, circumstances, and results for the one blessed with the boon of the star.

Little wonder then that few in snow-clad regions with freezing temperatures labelled him as Santa Claus, while those in temperate regions and the plains called the guardian angel by certain other names.

The lone festival known to the non-pagan-worshipping populace soon revolved not around the Father, the Son of the Holy Mother of all Creation, but as a mark of welcome to the Man of Love, suitor of the Princess of Stars, a Lone Ranger, so to speak. He was a Star Sage, warmth of love, a bridge between being celestial and human in the world we all live in.

So, let all the universe rejoice yet again. Pray in earnest. Reap your rewards. When the Almighty is your Guide, one does not require any mediator or medium for meditation, succour, and peace of mind. Share your laughter, so the stars too come to dance in your eyes.

And in those of all those around…!

16.

Sea of Love!

The cliffs jutted out along the mighty coast. The trees that dotted the coastline were tall, intimidatingly old, and their thorny leaves seemed like spears of the lance-wielding knights of yore! As the captain steered the course of his oil vessel towards the port, he noticed that amidst two huge rocks was the silhouette of a damsel who seemed to wear a coat of shining rose petals, lit by the setting sunlight and highlighted by the ring of golden light circling her flower-laden, long tresses. He even thought there were long snakes dangling from around her shining neck. But, being a seasoned sea-farer, he knew better than to be allured by illusions, and any illusion of a beautiful maiden always scared him stiff, for he knew that out of scores of such sightings reported, hardly a fraction were fairies, angels or mermaids, and all the rest were evil ghostly spirits, out in disguise as enchanting figures who were in fact out to hunt down weaklings and devour their blood as blue-blooded vampires do, so to speak!

He turned his gaze away only to see her arms swinging up across in the universal sign of 'help, help, I am in distress' – the 'save our souls' signal! Now, being a man who stayed sane despite the insane intake of countless bottles of rum and raw spirit, he realised that no gentleman seaman ought to ever ignore a distress cry, be it on high seas or on such islands! And the silver cross that his wife of two decades forced around his neck reminded him that divine help would come his way if the figure turned out to be an imposter ghoul! So, he blasted the foghorn of the ship in long bursts of acknowledgment and re-set the course of the vessel towards the inlet where the magnetic figure was beckoning.

In an hour, as he neared the shore, he commanded the three women sailors on board to go ashore, with three hefty, gun-wielding sailors as bodyguards, and stood up on the deck of his ship to monitor the operation. His mind wandered to the scores of rescues he had supervised in his illustrious career, firstly as Naval cadet, and then as an officer, and later on as the owner of a ship which was christened providentially as 'Manna of Life'. His train of thought was interrupted by the astonished cries of bewilderment of his crew members, and he saw that all the half a dozen strong rescue team were lying flat on their bellies on the sand dunes, and a few pine trees were crumbling down in their direction from a gust of wind which suddenly hit the region.

He walked down the steps from the sighting deck, ordered them all to make merry in the bar below, put on a visor and bulletproof vest and loaded his gun with ammunition, pulled a cowboy hat on, ambled along to the life boat and motored his way to the beach. Mentally prepared for the worst scenario, he said a prayer that his grandmother taught him on her lap as a young lad.

"Prayer power is always more helpful than gun power," the grand old dame would pontificate to the innocent, ignorant lad who did not even understand the meaning of a prayer, although guns and pistols hanging in the living room of their farm house always fascinated him!

As he leaped on to the shore, he moved away from the fallen folk, since his defence trainer had always screamed, "Don't you become sitting ducks' mates; duck away from the scene of war… evaluate, assess, fortify, plan, attack, emerge a winner, alive, and crush the foes!" He hid behind the foliage of some shrubs, from which little round fruits of different colours and shapes were all hanging – from the same mother plant! The next fifteen minutes were tense and long, with only his breath seeming to resound in the whole island body! He could then suddenly hear the sound of anklets coming from a north-eastern direction (looking at the compass on his wristwatch had become second nature for him). Peering through the small opening, he took notice of the terrain in that direction and was glad to see a natural formation of a tunnel by two rows of hanging branches of an unknown but green tree. He inched his way forward, thanking the sand for stifling the sound of his gumboots. After about half a mile, he heard the anklets loud and clear. The wearer of those anklets could be a jungle man with poisonous spear or arrow, but it may also belong to the beautiful maiden who hailed him from amidst the rocks. Alert as ever, he now crept slowly in between the tree-tunnel and adjoining rocks.

He was startled to suddenly come face to face with her! She was the most beautiful mermaid he had ever imagined or seen in any artwork! Even the beautiful full moon that was now lighting up the landscape paled in comparison, he mused. Much taller than his six-foot-tall, lanky frame, she was golden yellow and wore strange robes of rosé and crimson red, with pink as the defining shade, overflowing her form. A most delightful scent, which no perfumery could manufacture, was in the air around him.

Mustering up his courage, he looked up to meet her pearl like eyes and he noticed that she had a third eye, a diamond dazzling like no sun could ever do! And she held a staff like object, which on second glance he detected to be a long vine of silken texture, but completely covered by emeralds, rubies and corals. She had a lovely crown made of some unknown material, which somehow appeared to be of brilliant gold!

And then it occurred to him that there were more than two hands to the form: at least six more hands! Each held a different object: a pink lotus, a trident, a conch, a huge book, a discus. He could not see what were held by her remaining hands, for by then she was smiling at him as a mother would to her child! He was transfixed; he found himself unbuttoning the tunic and throwing the holster aside and he knelt in humble submission to the exalted apparition he thought was before him. But he found a general sense of calm and serene quietude about him. There was no fear within him, nor any show of hostility from outside.

He bowed with respect and found a blessing emanated in a melodic voice from whom he was now convinced was a Goddess, mystical or mythological: "Have you not been saying your prayer all these years, through stormy seas and high tides; through joys and sorrows; days and nights, morn after morn my child? Have you not been questioning your faith in your dear departed granny's prayer? Have you not called out loud to unseen, unknown almighty God seeking succour for many deprived souls around the globe? And have not the depraved minds called you names of ridicule for believing in God whom none of them have ever seen nor sought a glimpse of? Have you not been tending to that sick cook in your pantry of the ship, saying your prayers even as you attended to all other duties of your position? Have you not recounted the number of sumptuous meals and delicious fare he served you for long years and in gratitude prayed incessantly for a restoration of his good health?"

He could hear these words and sense these being translated to his native Yorkshire accent. He felt his eyes brim with tears. He knew not the reason, but felt his whole body trembling in relief, not excitement… He meekly nodded his head in agreement! How did this Goddess know it all? But aren't gods supposed to know all that happens inside a being's lifespan and even pave their way to the destiny of their lifetime?

"When you subscribe to the existence of good and bad; of evil spirits and good angels; of darkness and viruses or epidemics; of might of man and the inability of mankind to increase longevity – let alone making man immortal, what prevents you people from acknowledging the existence of Almighty God, a Supreme Force or Power, universal in nature – not confined to your prayer room or church, temple, synagogue, mosque or pagoda, but a God who resides in the heart of every human being and possessing multi-dimensional existence cutting across man made borders of nautical miles, leap years or United Nations and technological innovations…even in plants, animals and inanimate objects?"

The transfixed captain was catapulted from notions of being a much travelled, encyclopaedia of knowledge to but a microcosm of life as a human being. He lamely nodded his head in agreement.

The Goddess rested one of her palms on his head, and the soothing sensation at once reminded him of his mother and grandmother ruffling his locks of hair, and the nagging back pain which surgeons had pronounced as his chronic companion for a lifetime disappeared at once! He felt light and enlightened by the newfound knowledge of life, love and divinity. He found himself prostrating before Her magnificent form and 'worshipping' life, and the love of life itself was renewed in the sea-weary captain. The Divine apparition in turn flashed another quiet smile, and lo and behold, before he could raise his head again to look at the lovely Goddess, she disappeared.

He rose to his knees and ran around searching for the Goddess, but she was nowhere to be seen. His wireless radio crackled to life and his first officer was animatedly shouting aloud: "Captain, Sir, there is a marvellous toy in your cabin – shining, tiny and very primitive."

"Let that be as it is, Peter, I am coming over!"

As he neared his team of six, he saw them wake up as if from a stupor, and, freshened from a refreshing sleep, they danced around the captain, as they thought he was drunk and sporting the conical crown sitting atop his head!
Together, they all sailed back to the mother ship, and as the rejuvenated captain looked in amazement at the new appearance on his desk, he recognised the 'toy' to be an identical image of the Goddess, who touched him to galvanise him back to youthful thoughts and wiser actions!

The cook came rushing up to the engine room with an oriental delicacy – all were benumbed to see the sick and bed-ridden old man dish out a favourite fare, and in the pinkest of health.

As a huge wave lashed out at the window of the captain's cabin, he remembered the words of his grand old grandmother: "Sonny, Divinity is nothing but a sea of love: there is an Almighty God who blessed our Merchant Company by welcoming our buccaneer-tradesmen to the shores of her ancient land, but if you keep saying the prayer I have passed on to you, one fine day, God shall touch you and a new vision of world order, religious seas and ocean of life, it's purpose, meaning and purity will emerge: stay blessed dear!"

The rest of his life's journey was as an ambassador of the United Nations travelling around the world (in aeroplanes, not ships, for want of time) spreading the word of God: live in peace, harmony and build institutions of love, not hatred!

The twice-born!

17.

Roots of Love

(part one)

It was an irony of sorts that he felt a fiery desire engulf and become an obsession with him: the high school exams were over today, and he wished to visit the land of his roots – a remote village located amidst a dense forest in that much maligned land of the fakirs and poverty, as the mass media seemed to project, ever since he first heard of the name, India! An irony, because his parents and grandparents had not returned to the land of their birth ever since the paternal grandfather had migrated to the United States of America after topping at the famous MIT. His parents too were born in the adopted land and never seemed to harbour any desire to revisit the country of their ancestors. So free was the spirit of America that they had merged into the local cultural values and were community leaders respected by even the staff of the POTUS, it was widely believed.

Tomorrow was another day for the young lad: by the same yard-stick by which his great grandfather had permitted his grandfather to go abroad for higher studies, breaking the family tradition of taking to priesthood, an until then hereditary vocation taken up by every male offspring, his father too relented to his plea of visiting India and their native village during these vacations! But prior social engagements prevented his parents from accompanying him on the trip.

The high school principal had lectured to his class of the importance of 'knowing one's roots'! Being a bright pupil, he was the apple of his teachers' eyes: who doesn't like a winner? And, in such a free country as America, talent and industriousness were rewarded with applause, and all acknowledged healthy curiosity on all fronts, or so the youth believed! His request for a one-to-one discussion on the topic was accepted, and soon the decision was taken to visit the land of his family's origin and trace the roots of his heritage.

With all the newscasts of crimes occurring in that far away land of 'accented English' and 'barbaric mannerisms', he was being dissuaded by his mother from visiting her mother's motherland: but the explorer in her intelligent son sparked bright and begged her indulgence. Knowing his rights under law of the land, he even got his principal to have a telecon with his parents in order to get their assent to the trip.

***

As the flight landed, he was informed of his baggage having got lost at the stopover in a Middle Eastern airport famed for car races. Fortunately for him, the Principal had provided him with a letter of reference to an old Texas couple who had settled down at Agra, city of the Taj Mahal (a few hours' drive from Delhi, the national capital, he was told). The youth called up the couple, who were only too glad to inform him of an expressway from Delhi to Agra which required just a hundred odd minutes' drive to reach. And he found the road comparable to those home! The cab driver was courteous, and a pleasant drive took him home to his hosts, effortlessly.

After adequate rest, they took him around the old town and the famed landmark, which was simply stunning. He found the hustle and bustle of life around the cramped lanes and main roads as fascinating as a concert of Lady Gaga or Rihanna in their stadium. To his amazement, even bullocks and cows as well as dogs and donkeys were ambling along the highway in certain parts of the city. Signboards directed tourists and visitors easily and policemen stationed all across the city appeared to mingle with the never-ending surrounding traffic! There were roadside eateries, and then there were the most modern malls thrown in between old shuttered showrooms of sarees and other traditional garb of the local population. His only memory of a more crowded pace was the one day visit his family had made to Hong Kong, when he had assumed that flies were swarming at them instead of crowds of office goers in a hurry!

His baggage was delivered by the airline's staff in three days' time, and he took leave of his homeland hosts. This time, he boarded a train which would take him to Benares, believed even by Google's information to be the oldest living city in the world. The holy Ganges is a place he so yearned to visit, and even take a dip or swim if the waters of that mighty river invited him... and yes, of course, the swarm of human pilgrims permitting.

He was in for a bigger shock: it was the time of the Maha Kumbh Mela, a fair held once every twelve years, at the confluence of the mighty rivers of Ganges, Yamuna and a mystical third river, said to be dried up, called the Sarasvati. Millions of Hindu pilgrims converged and took a holy dip on the appointed dates and auspicious hours to ward off all sins in their lifetime and, as widely believed, to attain 'moksha' or salvation (thereby being rid of the cycle of rebirths, as Hinduism ordains). There were reportedly millions of people descending on the large banks of the river, and he was for a moment nonplussed when rickshawallahs, looking like thugs from a Hollywood flick on oriental themes, offered to give him a ride to the banks of the Ganges. However, on noticing the genuine affection and spirit of bonhomie and oneness of these volunteers, he reciprocated their disarming betel-leaf stained smiles. Soon, he mingled in the ocean of humanity.

Loudspeakers were blaring announcement after announcement about missing and lost persons, and others were playing devotional songs in the local Hindi language. But he stopped in his tracks upon reading a name board! He stepped into the tent and was amazed to meet a complete team of two hundred scholars from Harvard University, his father's alma mater, who had come down to study the Maha Kumbh Mela, the largest human religious meet, as they informed him! He found them all engrossed in animated conversations with Sadhus, press persons and other village folk, pilgrims all!

After managing to slip into the portion earmarked for these honoured guests from USA, and having had the luxury of taking a five-minute-long bath on the sacred occasion, the young man took another train to Hyderabad, down south in the central part of India, from where he was to undertake a bus journey to reach a small town bordering a forest, and then trek a few kilometres or take a horse carriage or bullock cart to reach his destination, the ancestral village.

***

As he stepped down from the air-conditioned bus on the outskirts of the Srisailam forest, he took note of a few startling facts.

Mobile phones were being widely used, so much so that even rag-pickers were clutching on to handsets! People were by and large wearing branded clothes and sporting the best of western fashion, even in rural parts. Huge signboards advertised off-season cuts on daily flights to New York, San Francisco, and Las Vegas. He was able to connect to his folks every other hour. His smartphone was behaving as gladly as if it were back in the States, although a wee bit slower, he mused! Men and women seemed to be equally free in their everyday activities, unlike all that one heard on news channels or witnessed in medieval lands visited in the recent past on school trips! The metro-rail and flyovers and most wondrous airport environment showed that India was no land of fakirs and nomads, but quite advanced as well as oriented with latest technological advancements of the western world! Apparently, there was a diabolical plan on the part of vested interests worldwide to lower the 'country-ratings' of this sub-continent. Unless India was technically capable, why would so much outsourcing take place from his lovely American land, and why else would the likes of his parents, grand parents and scores of other Indians be manning key positions across the spectrum of the modern world's most important bodies? The young boy was soon turning into a young man possessed of his own mind, over the course of this memorable journey!

But then, his smooth trip seemed to end, as he was informed at the forest department's check-post bordering the jungle that the road was closed, since there was an alarm of a tiger being on the prowl. It was believed to have strayed from its natural habitat in the hills dotting the horizon. And there was no inn or motel in this place! Not knowing what to do or where to go, he noticed the battery of his mobile phone was down and suddenly felt a wave of fear sweep over him.

The sun had set, it was dark and only a solitary temple was visible in the vicinity. He was not indoctrinated into the Hindu religion by his parents, but the interaction with the team from Harvard infused in him a faith and belief that this alien religion wasn't all about idolatry or pagan worship, but more of Spiritualism. It was by chanting "Govinda Hari Govinda," a mantra taught by these American scholars on the banks of the Ganges, that he mustered courage to push through the old iron gates and walk into the temple to take shelter for the night.

18.

Roots of Love

(part two)

There was nobody around. Three cows were tied to a neem tree, with a bundle of grass between them. They just cast a glance at the new visitor and resumed eating their fodder. There were flowers and garlands hung and a large iron bell dangling from the doorway. As he stepped towards the inner door, lit by three huge lamps glowing, he heard the sound of anklets which sounded almost like a musical fountain – but nobody was visible. He moved ahead slowly and halted as he came face to face with a smiling persona, whose eyes were shining, and crown bedazzled. He stood transfixed for what seemed an eternity, enamoured by the beauty of the magnificent presence before he pinched himself and said, "Shucks!" upon realising it to be the 'idol' in the temple. Being unversed with the local language, Telugu, inscribed on the old walls, apparently describing the deity's name, and since the smartphone wasn't functional, he couldn't look to Google Translate for help either!

But the pangs of hunger almost crippled his being. Not knowing what to do, he drank down the last drops of the mineral water bottle he was carrying. The sound of the trinkets or anklets continued. It was so musical that he almost forgot his hungry belly for a while. And then, his glance fell to a hand beckoning him from the image of the 'God' before him. There were four hands in all, he had observed in his initial stock-taking of this 'toy' these primitive people worshipped as God! He blinked non-stop on noticing that the hand was shining as if adorned in gold, and it soon began to look like his mother's hand, as it appeared whenever she used to hand-feed him back home. He cast a furtive glance towards the hand, and it was as if a real person was directing his attention towards a spot on the elevated table before him.

His mind told him to chant the mantra taught by his American brethren in the far away land of his ancestors, and to step forward and check out what was being shown to him. Lo and behold, there was a huge silver platter on which were arranged an array of the choicest fruits, sweetmeats, and a variety of local dishes that he had only seen on a computer screen while googling Indian cuisine… The child and the hungry young man in him got the better of him and he soon feasted upon the offerings. He also found a pitcher of sweet water and washed down his food with this nectar!

As often happens to a weary traveller, the good meal also made him feel drowsy. He spread out some huge, fresh banana tree leaves tied to the doorway and, removing his socks, tried to relax and have a good night's sleep. The flames of the two glowing lamps were dancing in the mild breeze, which sent in a draft of scented fragrance of exotic looking flowers and garlands that were dangling around the God's neckline. He tried to figure out the images being formed by the dancing flames. His thoughts then flew back to his home in the USA, and the fits which would visit his dear mom when he told her of having slept on an old marbled floor, sans air conditioning or mattresses, and in a dusty forest area where a man-eating tiger was on the prowl!

He smiled at the thought of her bewilderment. Dad, on the other hand, would just beam and wink at him. "Attaboy, the spirit of freedom always courted such adventures," Dad would declare…

He did not notice when he fell asleep but was awakened by the sound of musical trinkets and anklets of dancers. It was, he noticed, around 3 a.m. Local time on his wristwatch. But the lamps were no longer alight. The darkness around was dispelled by a group of luminous lights dancing in a circle around the Deity in the sanctum sanctorum. They appeared to be tall, lean, mesmerisingly enchanting, lovely, beautiful, and you could sense the joy, happiness and brightness of the atmosphere brought about by these 'figures'! All the seven (or nine? Or were they eleven?) he could sense were 'feminine forms'! Oh, the beauty of the sight was one to behold forever, a real treasure. Laser beams couldn't compare with these spirited, glowing lights!

Oh, the thought sent a chill down his spinal cord and he shut his eyes in fright of the unknown. His mind suddenly turned about face! What in the holy smokes was he doing in some primitive land alone, stranded in the middle of the night, and why could it not be ghosts in a spooky old building made of cobblestones, marble stone and rock? Did he blunder by venturing out, against his parents' caution, to a primitive land? Was he ever going to return home to the free world, safe and sound?

Even as these thoughts plagued him, he noticed a huge garland of red roses come flying out of the neck of the Deity towards his sleeping form, and as he sprang up to sit, he felt it land around his neck; that was the last waking thought he had, and he swooned into a deep slumber, only to be awakened by the sound of hand held bells, a conch and the beating of drums!

He opened his eyes to find the temple area lit by lamps and a dozen priests going around carrying out chores like giving a bath to the deity and arranging bowls of fruits, flowers, condiments, sweetmeats, and decorative leaves in and around the sanctum sanctorum. Outside, the first rays of a crimson red sun were sneaking through the foliage of the mango grove, and he wondered if Gods in this strange land of his forefathers' nativity woke up at such ungodly hours as 4 a.m.!

He tried to get up on his feet and was helped by an old priest donning the traditional attire of the locals (a dhoti, according to Google) and greeted with a benevolent smile. All the others congregated around him, and a couple of them even prostrated before him, to his utter shock. In halting Telugu, the local language he had picked up from his grandmother, he asked who they were and what were they up to?!

The elderly priest burst out laughing and spoke in flawless English, with a British accent: "Oh, but sonny, aren't you the one who has intruded into the Lord's sacred temple? But we salute you, because you are blessed, and pray, do tell me, how did you get to remove the sacred garland from Him and wear it around your neck? Weren't you afraid of sacrilege and sin?"

The astonished traveller recalled the scene and narrated the entire happening and, to his astonishment, he wasn't ridiculed, but believed at once. Then the head priest beckoned to three others and shot off a few instructions rapidly. In no time, the youth was escorted to a small cottage in the midst of a coconut grove and given fresh soap, warm water and a new pair of dhoti and angavastram to don after bathing. He experienced a new sensation of joy, warmth, and pride at being accorded such a humane welcome by totally unknown strangers in a strange, unknown part of the other side of the world to America! He could never imagine such a culture of hospitality existed!

After this, he was taken back into the temple premises and the sun began to shine bright as the 'arti' ceremony took place. Accompanied by the sound of drumbeats, a conch and a long flute-like instrument, hymns were recited and worship of the Deity practiced.

After the elaborate ceremony, he was beckoned by the elderly priest, who conversed in English and told him, "Sonny, I hear you are here to find your roots. This is very good. I happen to be your grandfather's cousin, who took over the hereditary duties of priesthood after he left for offshore fortunes. I am glad I am able to see you. Our village is about fifty kilometres from this temple, and you have to tread thirty by foot. Bears and leopards and other wild animals still roam around free in this jungle. There is a red alert about a maneater on the prowl, so, the single track is shut down by forest officials for a week at least..."

The young tourist was amazed at the unfolding of events before him and he was struck with awe at the whole scenario. His train of thought was interrupted by the booming voice: "...'There is an ancient tunnel leading up to the even more ancient, original temple built in the twelfth century BC. I shall not reveal to you the marvels of the place beforehand, but here, do eat these fruits and sweetmeats and I will show you the roots of the civilisation of the modern world itself, sonny!"

Hungry as he suddenly felt, the young man devoured the offerings and a fresh green mango fruit he leaped and plucked from a overhanging branch. Smiling at the young lad's innocence, the elderly priest then held a lantern and beckoned him to follow him. Ahead, two other young priests were clearing a passage for them through the thicket of bushes and wild growth!

After what seemed like an hour's wading through thorny bushes and fragrant flowers, and after leaping across rocks laid along a tiny stream, they entered another huge but solitary structure which resembled the newer temple in architecture, but smelt more like the Egyptian Pyramids his school had taken him to see on an excursion the year before!

Stone walls and then a huge image of an ancient God, made in black granite, it seemed, appeared before him. But then he halted, speechless as he espied a most amazing set of creatures moving about, slowly, at a snail's pace, it appeared! Wow…wow… wow! He whistled and yelled and leapt in mad rapturous delight! The old priest shushed him and held his hand.

"Sonny, yes, these are giant turtles which have a life span of ten thousand years. These were on planet Earth even before humans began a civilised lifestyle and religion was created by mankind!"

And the shock of the foreigner who came in search of his roots and, more, to investigate the heritage of his ancestors' native land grew by leaps and bounds. He could count at least a hundred giant turtles, larger than his lanky frame, smiling through their sleepy looking, heavy, beautiful bodies all around this ancient temple! They seemed undeterred by the presence of the intruders after the elderly priest sang out a hymn in the ancient language of Sanskrit, which is believed to be the mother of all Indian languages. Yes, this rang a bell in his Google-like mind – a German scholar had written a treatise that said ancient Sanskrit was the lingua franca of the Gods, and even German and other European languages had their roots linked to grammar of Sanskrit!

He then sought permission to click a few pictures but realised the battery of the iPhone had drained out the day before! He simply screamed, "Holy Cow!"

Then began the journey back to the modern world, and the only singularly interesting, though frightening, incident was when he witnessed a huge snake stretching at least fifteen feet fly across the huge, tall peepal and banyan trees in the valley!

Upon reaching the temple, he requested the hosts to explain the phenomenon of the night before, only to be hugged by the older priest, who had tears flowing down his kind, bearded face! After a few minutes of the emotional outburst, he said, "Sonny, you are most fortunate to have darshan (testimony) of God, the Divine, supreme, Almighty! You are blessed... Go, rise, shine in the world of your making. But, always remember, this is no make-believe Hollywood or Bollywood film. God is real. Divinity is Supreme, Universal. All that your nation exults in about rocket science, space technology, laser beams, is all buried in the wisdom of our ancient land. I will teach you a few lines, a verse in Sanskrit, which if and as you pronounce in the right way, and by practising vegetarianism and celibacy for at least two more decades, you would attain fame and help change the decadent societies of the world by becoming a minstrel of love!"

Then, he was ushered into the spot where he had slept the night before and given a mantra (ancient Sanskrit prayer), and then accorded a fond farewell by at least a hundred devotees, who had flocked from far and nearby hamlets on learning of the flying garland incident. They gave him plenty of gifts of the rarest of rare ornaments, fruits, and traditional garments to take home!

It is another story as to how he managed to memorise the mantra and convince the border security officials that he was not smuggling in diseases or viruses through these fruits and other sweetmeats, but carrying back home a piece of human civilisation itself! The Roots of Love, Harmony, Knowledge, Wisdom, Eternity itself!

It took him nearly three decades before he could share his emotive experiences with his parents, for they never had time together…until this day, when his daughter turned ten, and they had a family dinner on Christmas Eve, bound indoors by thick snowfall in the city of adoption!

The grandparents died without listening to his tryst with the Divine Lights, or those ancient giant Turtles which beamed at him!

Praise The Lord!

Long live mankind!
Blessed be Life!

19

Soul to Soul

I am liberated as a Soul, freed from a bodily form.

Yes, I was alive, living in the form of a human being.

I am dead, as they write, passed on to the next world.

And, they all say, Rest in Peace.

What was I?

In that life, born a Christian. Situations turned me to embrace another religion of Mankind. I became a Muslim. Occupation? I was a sportsman, a pugilist. Made my mark, early in life. Times were different from now. Fifty years ago, things were not different.

War and conflict. Differing views. Governance was not a societal affair, more a political dilemma of those at loggerheads with thinkers and literature.

I had won many encomiums, medals, prize monies. Fame was a knockout that jettisoned me to be labelled a legend.

In my supreme confidence level, I announced, "I am the greatest!"

They all cheered. Clapped. Repeated after me.

But I too suffered from all other needs and limitations of mortals. Eventually, I succumbed to illness. Here I am.

As a Soul.

As I witness all those memorial services, obituaries, and Twitter tributes, I am left without any feeling. Who am I?

I am not the greatest. Life is temporary. All temporal enjoyments indeed, temporary.

A mere passage of time, comprising of several acts, actions, deeds, misdeeds, misdemeanours, attempts at conquering a world where all are passengers in a journey they know not. To what end? And, for what purpose is such a relentless effort, generation after generation?

These thoughts confront me, now …

Souls have no birth. Nor death. We merely step in and step out. Those beings that show us courtesy lead a life of internal equanimity. Thoughts drive lifestyles.

Yes. Souls have no religion. No labels. Nor orders. Neither Books nor Leaders.

The Almighty decides where and when to depute a Soul, when to let a transcended soul be absorbed as a part & parcel of the Supreme Force.

We are Universe.

Only universal brotherhood, peaceful coexistence, and harmonious societies can let souls exist in peace whilst alive as creatures of Life.

Shun sinful existence. Look beyond Politicians. Eye a policy of truthful thoughts. Look beyond visible structures and advertisements of marketers. Live and let live. Souls rest in peace if let to live peacefully when they roam as living Beings on Earth.

Soul to Soul. This is the mode of communication.

Signed,

A Soul lost.

Life lost to the world. But, Souls win. A sublime Soul.

So, love All. Soul to Soul. Not by religion, caste, creed. These are creations. Artificial. Temporary. Divinity alone matters.

Even after matter ends lives...!

SEIN HERZ FÜR AUTOREN A HEART FOR AUTHORS À L'ÉCOUTE DES AUTEURS MIA ΚΑΡΔΙΑ ΓΙΑ ΣΥΓ
ΚΑΡΔΙΑ FÖR FÖRFATTARE UN CORAZÓN POR LOS AUTORES YAZARLARIMIZA GÖNÜL VERELIM SI
CUORE PER AUTORI ET HJERTE FOR FORFATTERE EEN HART VOOR SCHRIJVERS TEMOS OS AU
SZÍVÜNKÉRT SERCE DLA AUTORÓW EIN HERZ FÜR AUTOREN A HEART FOR AUTHORS À L'ÉCC
ORAÇÃO BCEЙ ДУШОЙ К АВТОРАМ ETT HJÄRTA FÖR FÖRFATTARE À LA ESCUCHA DE LOS AUT
TEURS MIA ΚΑΡΔΙΑ ΓΙΑ ΣΥΓΓΡΑΦΕΙΣ UN CUORE PER AUTORI ET HJERTE FOR FORFATTERE EEI
YAZARLARIMIZA GÖNÜL VERELIM SZÍVÜNKÉRT SERCE DLA AUTORÓW EIN HERZ F
SCHRIJVERS TEMOS OS AU ... ... AÇÃO BCEЙ ДУШОЙ К АВТОРАМ ETT HJÄRTA F

The author

Pamarty Venkataramana, an eminent jurist, poet, and thinker of the 21st century, has received the honour of being named the 'Prophet of New Age Literature'. 'The Whispering Star' is the first book of short stories he has published. His books of spiritual poetry – 'In A Blink', 'Chasing A Shadow' and 'A Master's Piece' – have been widely appreciated and run into many reprints.

The publisher

He who stops getting better stops being good.

This is the motto of novum publishing, and our focus is on finding new manuscripts, publishing them and offering long-term support to the authors.
Our publishing house was founded in 1997, and since then it has become THE expert for new authors and has won numerous awards.

Our editorial team will peruse each manuscript within a few weeks free of charge and without obligation.

You will find more information about novum publishing and our books on the internet:

www.novum-publishing.co.uk